Stonewall Inn Mysteries
Keith Kahla, General Editor

Sunday's Child by Edward Phillips
Death Takes the Stage by Donald Ward
Sherlock Holmes & the Mysterious Friend of Oscar Wilde
by Russell A. Brown
A Simple Suburban Murder by Mark Richard Zubro
A Body to Dye For by Grant Michaels
Why Isn't Becky Twitchell Dead? by Mark Richard Zubro
Sorry Now? by Mark Richard Zubro
Love You to Death by Grant Michaels
Third Man Out by Richard Stevenson
The Night G.A.A. Died by Jack Ricardo
Switching the Odds by Phyllis Knight
Principal Cause of Death by Mark Richard Zubro
Breach of Immunity by Molly Hite
Political Poison by Mark Richard Zubro
Brotherly Love by Randye Lordon
Dead on Your Feet by Grant Michaels
On the Other Hand, Death by Richard Stevenson
Shattered Rhythms by Phyllis Knight
Eclipse of the Heart by Ronald Tierney
A Queer Kind of Love by George Baxt
An Echo of Death by Mark Richard Zubro
Ice Blues by Richard Stevenson

An
Echo
of
Death

An
Echo
of
Death

Mark Richard Zubro

St. Martin's Press
New York

Library of Congress Cataloging-in-Publication Data

Zubro, Mark Richard.
    An echo of death : a Tom and Scott mystery / Mark Richard Zubro.
    p.   cm.
    ISBN 0-312-13480-0
    1. Carpenter, Scott (Fictitious character)—Fiction. 2. Mason,
Tom (Fictitious character)—Fiction. I. Title.
    [PS3576.U225E28   1995]
    813'.54—dc20   95-30299
                                                     CIP

First Stonewall Inn Edition: October 1995
10 9 8 7 6 5 4 3 2 1

◣◢ Acknowledgments ◢◣

For their kind help and patience: Barb D'Amato, Hugh Holton, Rick Paul, and Kathy Pakieser-Reed

An
Echo
of
Death

1

"And I don't want him there," I said.

"It's after two in the morning," Scott said. "Can't this wait until tomorrow?"

"No, I want to talk about it now."

I glared out the window of the cab toward the Salvation Army Headquarters at Addison and Broadway. After the light changed, the driver waited for oncoming traffic to clear, then turned left and sped toward Lake Shore Drive. The cabbie's radio crackled for a few seconds. Then all I heard was the swish of tires on the rain-misted streets.

"Tom, he's a friend," Scott said. "He needs help."

Even with the glass partition between us and the cab-driver nearly closed, we spoke in hushed voices.

"He's an overgrown child with a drug habit whose family owns half of this city," I said. "Why didn't he run to Mommy and Daddy for help?"

"He didn't say," Scott admitted.

"And that's another thing I don't like," I said. "He hasn't explained what this so-called big trouble is. We're supposed to simply believe him that something bad happened in Mexico, he rushed up to Chicago and came straight to us, and we've got to protect him and he can't tell us why? He probably tried smuggling drugs into the country and got caught or is about to get caught, and your reputation is going to be ruined along with his. He'll be suspended for life—again."

The driver turned his wipers to intermittent as we waited for the traffic signal at Addison and Lake Shore Drive. Outside the cab, the light drops of moisture sprinkled themselves on black puddles.

Scott said, "He promised me he was clean, and he said he could tell us the whole story. He just needs a little more time."

"He also has a habit of exaggerating," I said. "Remember the time he got everybody on the team feeling sorry for him because he said he might have cancer? Turned out to be an exceptionally large boil."

"I know he likes attention," Scott said, "but something about the way he talked last night made me believe him. I'm really upset about the way you treated him. At least he tried to be pleasant, and you didn't need to sneer at the gift he gave you."

"They've got to be fake, or at least we better hope they are." Glen Proctor had given us each a necklace for a gift. He had claimed that the stone at the center of Scott's necklace was a Colombian emerald. It was the size of a quarter and the deepest green you could possibly imagine, and he swore the rest of the necklace was Mexican gold which was studded with diamonds, some the size of dimes. Mine had a stone that he claimed was a ruby but seemed mostly purplish and opaque to me.

"If those things are real," I said, "they are worth hundreds of thousands of dollars, and he wouldn't be giving them to us. A real possibility is that he stole them, and by giving them to us, we're put in danger. It's not like we exchange birthday and Christmas gifts. This is out of the blue, and I don't like it."

"We can have a jeweler appraise them," Scott said.

"A gemologist."

"Huh?"

"You need a gemologist to appraise stones like this. Most jewelers don't know the first thing about . . ."

"Fine," he said. "We'll get the King of Persia or whoever you want to play with the jewels. My point is, you could have been more polite when he gave it to you. It wouldn't have killed you to say thanks."

"I'd rather buy a watch off a guy peddling them in the street. I'd trust him more than I trust Glen Proctor." Actually, I thought I'd been reasonably grateful—or at least tried to be.

"You're not being fair," Scott said.

"They're gaudy and they look stupid," I said. Scott had chosen to wear his this evening. "You look like a reject from a disco that's been nuked." I had tossed mine in the bottom of a drawer, hoping it would disappear forever.

Scott was still trying to be relatively reasonable. He hadn't gotten to short, clipped sentences yet. We hadn't had time for this conversation last night or earlier today. Scott had stayed up until the early hours talking to Glen. I hadn't wakened when he'd come to bed. I'd had to go out for most of the afternoon to run some errands that I'd promised to do for my parents. We'd argued briefly while dressing for the fund-raiser, but Glen's hovering around prevented a major fight. We'd driven to the dinner in reasonable civility. On the way home, I had broached the subject as soon as the cab started away from the curb. He was trying to be calm and reasonable, neither of which I felt at the moment.

Scott touched the chain that barely peeped from beneath the loosened tie and opened top button of his shirt.

"People change," Scott said.

"I don't like him," I said.

"You're jealous," Scott said as the driver cut off two other cars to be the first up the on ramp to Lake Shore Drive.

"I find it strange that he just happened to manage to

walk around the apartment in the most clinging underwear this noon and accidentally rub up against you when you passed in the hall, and that he practically sat in your lap while leaning over your shoulder when you were reading the paper. If he'd been any closer while you were making toast, he'd have come out singed, and he wears too much after-shave. It's not as if there isn't enough room in the penthouse for an army. He didn't have to get that close."

Glen Proctor's underwear had been molded around his taut butt and bulging crotch. The guy had the compact muscular body of a stud athlete that I would have cheerfully shoved off the top of the building.

"He's straight," Scott said. "He brags about all his conquests with women. Every chance he gets, in the locker room, on the field, on the bus and everywhere else, he tells us how great he is with women."

"And that's another thing," I said. "Besides being a prick tease, the man is a menace. That kind of promiscuity is unforgivable."

"You don't know whether he uses protection."

"How can you defend him?" I asked.

We were talking about Glen Garrison Proctor III, one of the phenoms of the last few baseball seasons. He'd openly bragged last night that he wanted to break Steve Howe's record for being suspended for life from baseball the most times.

Proctor and Scott had been teammates during Glen's first and second years in the majors. They'd become close friends, and Scott had been the players' union rep during Glen's suspension and before he was traded after the second season. They wound up working together for hours that year on Glen's first dismissal from baseball.

"I defend him because he's my friend. I'd think you'd be more understanding."

"I wish I could be, but I think he's dangerous. You don't know what-all trouble he's gotten himself into. I didn't like him the first time I met him, and I still don't like him. He takes from people and never gives. He is the most self-indulgent person I've ever met, and I don't know why you can't see it. Frankly, I think we should call the police. He's nuts and he's stupid."

"You're wrong," Scott said. "You're being unfair, and I don't like it. You always call something stupid when you're the one who doesn't understand. You're the one with the problem."

The rest of the drive to Scott's penthouse occurred in icy silence.

Out of the cab, Scott slammed the door and swept ahead of me toward the entrance. Howard, the night doorman, didn't greet us with his toothy smile. He was probably on one of his numerous breaks or occasional real errands. Seemingly a thousand times a night, Howard found excuses to attend to everything but his job. I always figured he hid in some dark corner to grab as many naps as he could when he should have been on duty. Scott had to use his key to let us in the lobby entrance. Howard locked it if he wasn't standing at his post, and tenants knew to use their keys. I caught up with Scott while he fussed with the door, but he ignored me as he marched across the lobby to the elevators. He punched the heat-sensitive button fiercely.

I trailed through the marble-encrusted entry, feet clicking on the highly polished floor. We'd been to a fund-raising dinner for a lesbian candidate for alderman in the 44th Ward. It hadn't helped my mood any when the gay people in the audience fawned over my lover from the minute we entered the room. Yes, I know he was the main reason many of them bought tickets. I seldom have a problem with his fame, but being completely ignored by the crowd, coming on top of Glen's presence back home, increased my anger.

Scott inserted the special key that allowed the elevator to deliver us to the penthouse. We barely glanced at each other while we rode to the top floor. Off the elevator and across to the only door on this floor, we remained silent.

Inside he flicked on the foyer light and stalked through the entryway and then turned left toward our bedroom. I hung my black leather jacket in the hall closet and began loosening my tie as I strode through the foyer and turned right into the living room.

In the hallway, I tripped over a pile of boards and a scattering of bricks. Glen Proctor had been the proximate cause of our morning squabble, but his presence had only exacerbated a month-long difficult time in our relationship. My home had burned down several months earlier. We'd lived together at either Scott's place or mine for years, but we'd never consolidated households. This was at my insistence. The issue was dependence. Scott is one of the highest-paid pitchers in baseball, and something in my pride said that moving in with him would be a kind of living off his income and a loss of my independence. But after the fire, a series of discussions had resulted in a huge compromise. We would redecorate his place, and I would move in permanently.

It sounded so simple, but all his money made it worse. Scott—and thus we—could afford just about anything we wanted. First of all, we've always used separate bathrooms. I love watching him shave and his double-nozzle sunken tub and Jacuzzi were very sexy, but I'm a slob and he's a neatnik; and yes, I know he's got a maid service, but if he put my stuff onto my shelf in my cabinet one more time, I was going to toss it through one of the floor-to-ceiling windows.

This week's epic battle had been over the bathroom faucets. He wanted gold-plated ones made in Italy. This made no sense to me. And the whole operation would have a waterfall effect for the flow in the sink in each bathroom, a soft and gentle cascade of fluid. Very nice, but how are you supposed to rinse the toothpaste from your brush or the hair from your razor in a gentle flow? He couldn't understand why mine had to be different from his.

It did seem like the smaller and less significant the item became, the more we fought over it. What I really wanted to do—and more so with each grapple with contractors and fight over minutiae—was to build a new place down in the south suburbs near where I taught high school. I knew I loved him and I wanted our relationship never to end, but I had to tell him soon that I wanted my own place. We'd go on as we had before, living together in my place or his.

I passed the mountain of mess in the hall, strode a few feet forward, and tripped over the debris left by the workers renovating the fireplace in the living room. Arguing about this (what kind of stone and how large) had long since taken backseat to arguing over who was going to call which day to find out where the hell the workmen were. They'd promised to finish the job twenty-six days ago, but who's counting? At their speed, they might be finished before the next ice age. We'd fought about who would move the beginnings of the soon to be fireplace out of the way so we'd stop running into it.

I pulled myself up and dusted off my hands and paused in the entrance to the living room. I usually paused to survey the fantastic view of Chicago's magnificent buildings that could be seen through the walls of glass windows. But now I also paused to try to let my anger cool. Watching the towering works of man always had a soothing effect on me. I sighed at the quiet majesty, descended two steps, and stopped.

On the far side of the room, propped up against the windows and sitting three feet to the left of the table that held Scott's baseball trophies was Glen Proctor. He had a large red stain in the center of his beige fisherman's sweater. A small red pool around his body showed starkly against the white carpeting.

"Scott!" I called while I hurried to the body. A bullet between Glen's eyes had penetrated but not emerged against the glass. A smear of blood and a rim of black showed around the wound. Splashes of blood dribbled from both sides of his nose. The gaping hole in his chest told of the source for the still-damp blood pooled on his chest.

"Scott!" I called again.

Proctor was dressed in the usual tight acid-washed Levi's he always wore, the type that emphasized the bulge in his crotch, and the round firmness of his butt. I didn't say he wasn't attractive, just that I didn't like him. He wore dark mahogany loafers and beige socks.

I checked for a pulse, although I didn't think there was much point. As I touched the cool skin around his neck, the memory of similar contact with bodies in the jungle while in the marines in Vietnam flashed through my mind. The instant my fingertips made contact with his skin, they confirmed the obvious, but I moved my hand up to the flesh over the carotid artery. A few seconds there absolutely confirmed that the handsome and swaggering Glen Proctor wouldn't play another inning of baseball.

I glanced around the room. Where was Scott? Fear chilled every bone in my spine as I realized the killer might still be in the penthouse.

I whirled around trying to sense any alien smell, sound, or sight. Nothing else in this room seemed out of place, but with the mess from the workmen, it was hard to tell. I tiptoed noiselessly toward the hall down which Scott had disappeared. Five feet before I turned the corner, I eased up against the wall. I listened intently, but even the heaviest footfall would be muffled by the inches thick carpet. I debated which way to sneak through the warren of rooms in the penthouse, but I didn't know from which direction an enemy might appear. Most of all, I wanted to find Scott and make sure he was all right. I drew a silent breath and swung out toward the hallway to the bedroom and almost banged into Scott.

"What the hell's going on?" he asked. "I heard you calling. Glen's not around."

For a comment I pointed across the room.

Scott looked. "What happened?" he said. "Is he . . ."

"Glen's dead," I whispered. "The killers could still be in here."

"We've got to call for help," he whispered back.

I pushed Scott up against the wall next to me. "We've got to be careful," I said.

That's when the knocking started on the front door.

Scott turned toward the noise, then glanced back at the body and said, "I'll get the door."

"No," I whispered. "How could anybody get up here? Only you and I have keys for this stop on the elevator."

"Howard has a key," Scott said.

"He wasn't at his post, and he wouldn't give out his key to a stranger. He'd have called up here first."

"Who's there?" Scott called out.

The knocking changed to shouts of "Open up! Police!" Then I heard thuds, as if someone was trying to break open the door.

"We're getting out of here!" I said.

"It's the police," Scott said. "We can't run!" He began to move toward the entryway. I stopped him at the far end of the hall, from which we could see the front door.

"Something is not right," I said. I grabbed his arm and began pulling him along. "Let's go out the back way. We can talk to the cops when we get downstairs. This is too spooky. Come on!"

Someone started banging repeatedly on the door. Then somebody shouted, "Hold it!" A few moments of silence followed. The doorknob slowly began to turn.

"Let's go!" I said.

Reluctantly, he began to follow.

Suddenly the front door crashed open. Men carrying machine guns and sawed-off shotguns leaped through the opening. That was more firepower than your ordinary beat cop or police detective in Chicago carried.

I shoved Scott out of the line of fire and leaped after him. "Not cops! Run!" I yelled.

Galvanized into action, we tore through the 8,000 square feet of twists and turns of the penthouse.

The elevators rose in the middle. You walked out of them facing east and proceeded to enter the complex down a hallway to a living room. Off this to the right through louvered doors was a den through which you could get to a library, all of which faced north. To the left of the living room was the kitchen area that faced east.

You could make a circuit three-quarters of the way around the outer rim of the penthouse. The bedroom with its matching bathrooms was completely cut off from the circuit and covered most of the western wall looking toward the prairies of Illinois and beyond.

The exterior rooms tended to be long and expansive, with great views of the city or lake. One guest bedroom beyond the den afforded a fantastic panorama of city and sky. The other rooms all branched off an interior corridor.

We tore through the kitchen to the interior hallway. The rehabbers had been busy here, removing one wall to help make the television room and a small bedroom into one large suite for all the electronic paraphernalia I liked to have around. Scott tripped over a stack of two-by-fours. I tumbled into him.

He cried out. I jumped up. His body had cushioned my fall, but my elbow had caught him in the nuts. I helped him up. His hands covered his crotch and he moaned.

I jammed two-by-fours between the wall and the door to construct a barrier between them and us. I heard banging on the door, but the hastily wedged two-by-fours held for the moment. If these guys took a minute, they would find another way through the warren of the penthouse and arrive at us from the opposite direction. We couldn't stay here.

"Let's go," I said.

Scott breathed deeply several times.

"Can you run?"

He nodded. He staggered for a few feet and then began to move with more confidence.

We rushed to the stairs that led to the floor below where Scott had installed a private gym with a running track around the perimeter and thousands of dollars of the most up-to-date training equipment in the middle.

We crossed quickly, dodging between machines and barbells. At the exit door, I looked back to see the killers just emerging at the far edge of the running track. Quickly through the door, we began descending flights of stairs. The rear entrance existed specifically because of fire-code regulations.

We passed numerous fire doors leading to the floors we hurtled past. We didn't dare try opening one of these emergency doors leading to the inhabited floors we flew by. Who knew whether we'd run into someone willing to help, and we could spend precious seconds banging on doors trying to find someone who was home. Besides, getting into somebody's apartment and holding up until whoever this was bashed down that door didn't seem to make much sense. Or we might wait who-knows-how-long for an elevator and could be trapped in the hallway. So far we had no evidence of enemies coming up from below us.

We flew pell-mell down. Around the fifteenth floor, Scott stumbled.

I grabbed him. "You okay?"

"Yeah. What if they're waiting for us at the bottom?"

"I don't know. Go!"

In the brief pause, I heard the pounding footsteps above us.

It didn't help that we were both still in our dress shoes. The soles made the going more slippery and kept me from hitting top speed.

Gasping great gulps of air into my seared lungs and willing my tired legs to keep going, we ran on, finally arriving at the ground floor with pursuit still far behind us but coming on quick. We both worked out, and Scott, a professional athlete, was in great shape; so even with the wrong type of shoes, we probably gained in the rush down.

At the foyer level we were now on, the stairs ended at the rear of a room that once had been a lounge for guests and tenants to meet. It hadn't been used as such since the seventies, when the new marble-and-glass front of the building had replaced an art deco eyesore or treasure, depending on whose side of the fight over the change you'd been on. I could see old couches, table lamps, and oil paintings by deservedly unknown artists. Huge canvas cloths covered nearly half of the relics of a lost golden age. With all this debris, the thirty-by-forty-foot space was tough to maneuver through. Near the front were a row of buckets, carpet cleaners, mops, brooms, and cardboard boxes labeled: INDUSTRIAL STRENGTH SEE INSTRUCTIONS ON CONTAINER.

An exit to our immediate left led I knew not where. A door twenty or thirty feet straight ahead of us led to the foyer. Through its square of glass, I could see the front desk. Howard wasn't present, but I saw the top half of a bald man with a blond mustache speaking into a portable phone. He clicked it shut and motioned toward the door I was looking through.

"They're coming this way," I said. "No choice." I led us to the door on the left.

As I pulled on the handle, the door to the foyer banged open.

"Get them!" the bald man yelled.

I yanked on the door. It was stuck or locked. I glanced over my shoulder. Two guys had joined Baldy. One was pulling a gun. Scott leaned down, and we both yanked on the handle. It burst open.

It was a straight flight down maybe twenty stairs with one bulb overhead illuminating cinder blocks painted white. Down we rushed. I wrenched open the door at the bottom. Scott leaped through and I darted after him.

I wondered why they didn't shoot. They wouldn't get the best shot, but all the way down the endless flights from the penthouse, that threat had flashed through my mind.

We arrived at the underground parking garage. The lighted security area loomed fifty feet on the other side of the car-filled underground barn. Two hefty looking guys in gray suits glared at the surrounding cars from within the glow of the neon of the glassed-in enclosure. They looked very much like the guys upstairs and definitely not like the blue-jean-clad casual guys who parked the cars and were our supposed security. These two guys held their hands inside their vests, maybe pretending they were Napoleon, or maybe ready to reach for their guns. They were between us and my pickup truck or Scott's Porsche; but, even more important, between us and the ramp leading out.

A car started up on our left and moved toward us. I decided not to wait around to see if it was someone barreling down on us trying to run us over or simply somebody on their way out.

"We can't get past them," Scott said. "Now what?"

I pointed to the ramp leading to the bottom level. "That way," I whispered.

"Can we get out that way?" Scott whispered back.

"I hope so," I said. "The only other way is blocked."

For some reason, I desperately wanted to say, "Walk this way," and a brief vision of old comedies flashed in my mind. You think of the goofiest stuff at scary times.

Forcing my tired legs to move, I started jogging toward the car-sized opening that led down. The door we just exited banged open behind us.

"Where are they?" someone shouted.

I glanced behind and saw the guys at the security desk running over to join the newly emerged guys from the stairs.

As we rushed around the corner leading to the next level, I heard a set of brakes squeal, a male voice swore, and someone shouted, "There they are!"

We flew down the ramp and entered another flat parking expanse jammed with cars. This area was darker because there was no illumination from a security area. Neon lights gave off their impersonal emanations at regular intervals. No people or cars moved at this level.

I raked my eyes over the gray walls searching for an opening. On the opposite wall away from the ramp leading up, an exit sign glowed redly. No time for indecision. I had no idea where this new doorway led, but we couldn't go back.

We hunched behind cars and ran bent over. They would see the one exit sign, too, but they couldn't be sure which way we were taking to get there. Maybe they'd split up to hunt for us among the cars. I'd have preferred a vast suburban mall parking lot for them to spread out and search.

My muscles were long since past aching from the race down the stairs, but I urged them to further efforts. I'd seen the results of these guys' ministrations on Glen Proctor, and I didn't imagine gaping red holes in various parts of my anatomy would improve my appearance.

Scott trotted ahead of me. I could hear his rasping breaths. Ten feet away from the new opening, I saw Scott glance back. "At the end of the ramp," he gasped.

I didn't bother to look back. I leaped forward. I shoved on the safety bar on the door. We emerged onto a five-foot-by-five-foot landing with stairs leading down to the left, with a single bulb enmeshed in a wire screen providing illumination. The air smelled dank and unused. Down the stairs we rushed to another landing which contained two gray doors perpendicular to each other, one in front of us and one on our left. Both had large gothic lettering saying "Do Not Enter."

Scott banged open the one in front. Over his shoulder, I saw it was crammed with buckets, mops, brooms, pails, and cleansers. I pulled open the door on the left.

We paced slowly for a few seconds down the narrow center aisle of a room lit by widely spaced bare bulbs encased as the one on the landing had been. To our immediate right was a freight elevator whose gaping maw was enclosed by a row of wooden picket teeth, joined in the middle. The cage wasn't on this level. We could see into a mass of cables that seemed to end in the depths about ten feet below where we were.

Beyond this on the right and to our left the room spread out, but I couldn't see how far the walls extended because cardboard boxes stacked nearly to the ceiling barred any vision in those directions. The boxes had labels such as "light bulbs," "plumbing fixtures."

The path stretched for another hundred feet and ended in a row of boxes. No indentation led off to right or left. We hurried toward the far end hoping for some way out. I began to lose hope as we passed between the looming walls of brown.

As we hurried down the path, we swiveled our heads in every direction trying desperately to spot any escape. It was useless to try hiding in a box. They knew we'd come down here. The prospect of searching even this many boxes wouldn't deter them, not with the kind of determination this crowd seemed more than likely to have.

No opening appeared among the rows of boxes.

"There!" Scott pointed.

I looked. The row of lights ran above the central corridor, but to our left near the far end about fifty feet away, a feeble light glowed in the murky dimness. Because of the boxes, we couldn't see what it illuminated, but there had to be a reason for its being back there, and we were rapidly running out of choices. We hurried forward. We reached the end of the box-induced hallway. No path led to the light. The door behind us crashed open.

We scrambled up a staircase of boxes. At the top it was impossible to stand up, so we alternately crab-walked or crawled toward the light. Several times my back or butt touched the clammy ceiling, which I could feel through my shirt and pants. The boxes must have been full because, as we scrambled forward, while we heard faint crunches and made occasional dents in the packaging, neither hand nor foot penetrated the outside. Perhaps we were moving fast enough so as not to put sufficient pressure for one of us to fall through. This cardboard flooring held until we scrambled down the far side, half sliding, then falling. My foot sank into one of the boxes, and I began to lose my balance. I growled in frustration. Scott reached back and hauled me up. We jumped past the last set of boxes to the floor.

The feeble glow we had seen illuminated a little square of space fronted by two doors. In bold red letters, one said "High-Voltage Electricity, Keep Out." I yanked it open. A million wires glared back at me.

Cardboard cartons began being shoved around behind us. Looking back, I saw the head and gun of one of our pursuers emerge as he slid toward us over the barrier of boxes. He leaned on a carton beneath him with his left hand and with the other raised his gun and pointed it at us.

"Hold it, you two!" he bellowed.

The carton he was resting his weight on gave way. His left arm disappeared up to the elbow. The arm with the gun shot up toward the ceiling, and the weapon fired.

The noise and smell surrounded us, but I had no time for that. The other door said "No Admittance." Scott had already ignored the sign and was through the opening. I followed, closing the door behind me.

2

Pitch-black. Midnight on the ocean. Negative on the hand in front of your face, too. I felt Scott's palm against my chest. "Hold it! I at least saw that we've got a flight of stairs here. Be careful," Scott said.

I inched forward, found the step, and started down. Scott was on my right. With my left hand, I felt the cool brick wall. We had carefully clambered down twenty-five stairs when the door above swung open. The glow wasn't very bright, and we had been deprived of light for only a short while so our eyes didn't wince at the new light. It let us see enough to dash a few more steps to the bottom of what was a narrow set of stairs. An opening at the bottom turned abruptly to the left, and we found one more set of stairs.

In the shadowy light, with the sound of footsteps pounding behind us, we fled down again. At the bottom were two passageways, both opening into total blackness. I grabbed the sleeve of his shirt and pulled him toward the opening on the left.

No shouts or gunshots followed. I listened as we hurried along. I heard no sounds of pursuit. Perhaps they hadn't been close enough to see which way we took, and now they would be as blind as we were.

As the dim glow behind us rapidly dwindled, I slowed

slightly to breathe more easily. I didn't want to trip over something as the light failed.

"I don't know how much more of this I can take," Scott said. His voice reverberated in the passage.

"Hush," I said and needed to say no more. He'd heard the echo of his own voice as well as I.

We paced rapidly until the light behind us was the size of a pinprick. I held out a hand for Scott to stop. I slumped against the wall on my left and listened to the two of us breathe. Not another sound came from anywhere.

"Are they following us?" Scott asked.

I blinked back to where the last vestige of a gleam had been. I couldn't tell whether the pinprick of illumination swayed as a light would if carried by someone, or whether it was simply a light at the beginning of the tunnel.

"I don't know," I said. I let myself pant for another minute, ears straining for any sound of movement behind us.

"Where are we?" Scott asked.

"Don't know."

I heard his breathing begin to become more even.

Despite the rapidity of our progress and the fast-fading light, I managed to take some note of our temporary place of existence. The floor and walls of the passage we were in were cement. The floor was damp with frequent puddles of water that we plowed through. Each side curved to meet about a foot or so above our heads. Several sizes of pipe ran along the roof. We could walk or run side by side. Each outside elbow would scrape against a wall. The exact center of the tunnel gave us plenty of vertical room. Because we were moving side by side, our heads nearly scraped the sides of the excavation. The air felt cold and damp, but there was no wind.

"Awful dark," Scott said.

"Unless they've got flashlights, it works against them and *for* us, I think."

"Maybe they took the other turn," Scott said. "I don't know if they saw which way we went."

"If we're lucky, they didn't."

My breathing wasn't back to normal yet, but I whispered, "I don't want to stop here any longer. I think we should keep going forward. This has got to lead somewhere."

"I hope!" Scott said.

We pushed forward, and in a moment all vestige of possible light was gone. We tried to keep our footfalls silent, but I was still in my dress shoes and they clicked with what was probably a minor tap, but which after a time, I thought was firecracker loudness. Scott had dressed far more casually than I for the fund-raiser, which meant he'd worn chinos, a pale yellow shirt, blue blazer, and brown dress shoes. He still wore everything except the blazer.

Our steps became more hesitant as we went along. So far we hadn't run into any obstructions, but I had no idea whether sudden openings would gape in the floor, or whether we'd run into a flight of stairs. In a short while, we were slowly groping forward, with feet and fingers extended ahead and to the side of us. Careful as our movements were, we still managed occasionally to dislodge what I guessed to be small stones or pieces of wood. They echoed slightly, but we could hardly help running into them. So far no creepy critters or crawly insects had decided to make their presence known. The place smelled as if someone hadn't emptied their cat-litter box in years.

At one point, I tried counting the number of paces we took, but gave it up after a couple of hundred. Certainly we were traveling some distance. The tunnel seemed to go on straight. If we needed to go back, it wouldn't matter how far we walked. We could just turn around.

I couldn't see the face on my watch, so I don't know how long it was after I stopped counting when Scott said, "I'm scared."

"Me, too," I said.

We felt our way forward for a few more steps. Then Scott said, "I'm sorry about bringing Glen into the house. You were right. He was into something awful. It's my fault we're in this."

I wanted to say, "I told you so, and you should have listened," but this was not the time. When we were safe again, I could indulge in my frustrations. I muttered a non-committal "S'okay."

If we decided to compare our insights or lack thereof about mutual acquaintances, although none of mine had gone this spectacularly wrong, Scott could remind me about our problem with the dwarf, the psychic, and the buffalo five years ago, when we encountered the above-mentioned at the height of the worst monsoon storm in Bombay in thirty years. All I had to do that day was agree to stay in the hotel room until afternoon. My insistence on going out had lead to a classic disaster. Memory could never blur the sheer terror of the events that followed; but, in my opinion, it hadn't been nearly as life threatening as this. At the present moment, I didn't want to stop and ask Scott's opinion of that escapade.

We fumbled onward for a time. Occasionally his right and my left arms, shoulders, or knees, bumped together. After one such movement, I felt Scott's hand slip into mine. I drew immense comfort from that closeness. I on the right, using my right arm, he on the left using his left, groped our way along the wall. Hand in hand we shuffled forward.

Our progress felt glacial, but although nothing sounded behind us, my fear began to grow. I'd never had trouble with claustrophobia before, but being this far under-ground, with fear behind us, and uncertainty ahead, I was upset big-time. Without Scott's presence, I don't know how I would have managed.

Scott said, "I think there's a light ahead."

We stopped. "You're right," I muttered.

Scott asked the obvious question. "What could it be?"

"I don't know, but we'd better be careful until we're sure."

"They couldn't get ahead of us?" Scott asked.

"If they've got lights, they could, and if the opening we didn't take eventually led this way."

It took several moments for the pinprick of light ahead to swell to the size of a baseball, but its glow barely penetrated to our position. It began to look like a miniature train-engine light bobbing in the distance. I halted for a moment; then my good sense chased away the irrational thought that it was a train. There were no rails under our feet, and any sound of thundering wheels would have echoed throughout the tunnel.

"Should we go back?" Scott whispered.

"We know for sure they're behind us somewhere," I murmured. "We've got to try forward."

Cupping my hands around my mouth and placing my lips against his ear, I explained to Scott how we needed to move. I felt his ear brush against my lips as he nodded that he understood. Each footfall now became a slow-motion quest for noiselessness. We raised each foot deliberately off the floor, moved it several inches farther down the hall, then placed it slowly into nothingness until it touched the concrete with less than a feather's murmur.

The gleam from in front of us had ceased to move. Perhaps my eyes had played tricks on me and the light had never moved, or maybe it was just my fears that had made it seem to bob and weave.

Around fifty feet from the source of the illumination, I touched Scott's shoulder. He stopped. I wanted to do a lot more observing and evaluating before moving closer.

What had seemed like the glow from a thousand-watt bulb, I now guessed must be the feeble glimmer from a rapidly fading flashlight. We heard voices, barely kept low.

"Are you sure we're ahead of them?" a baritone voice asked.

A tenor responded, "They don't have a light. They have to be moving carefully."

"Maybe they just ran," Baritone said. "They could be past us," he insisted.

"Not possible. With a light we could move much faster and this was the first junction."

"Maybe they found another junction somewhere on their side that led off in another direction. We had one." Baritone's deep voice had an unattractive whine mixed in with it.

"I say we stay here," Tenor said. "The other guys said they'd go back for more flashlights and follow the other passageway. If there's another turn, we'll get more men. Those two guys will be trapped between us and them."

Obviously, we couldn't simply outwait them. Reinforcements would be coming, and we'd be stuck.

I could make out only the outlines of shadows leaning against the far wall. I could attach no face or feature to their floating voices.

"I don't like it," Baritone said.

"You want to start going against my decisions?" Tenor voice asked.

Baritone added a bit of sullen to his whine, "No. I just don't like being this far underground and these tunnels flooded once before."

Now I knew where we were.

On April 13, 1992, tons of water broke through the walls of the tunnel system that runs under Chicago's Loop. Water had gushed from the Chicago River into the basements and subbasements of hundreds of buildings. The water used the old tunnel system as a conduit for its flow.

The tunnels, built between 1899 and 1909, originally were a roadway for small electric trains making deliveries—usually coal—to Loop buildings. The train company went bust in the 1950s, and then in the 1970s utility companies began using the tunnels instead of digging up city streets to lay cable. Most of the rails had been cemented over. The city planned to install bulkheads and steel doors to seal off tunnel sections under the river to prevent any further flooding, but in such a way as to let the advanced technology of the future still use the old system.

22

I remembered that there had been more than fifty miles of tunnels. The first shaft had been sunk in the basement of a saloon at 165 West Madison Street.

Concrete had been applied along the walls to give them a smooth, finished appearance. Generally the opening was 6′9″ wide and 7′6″ high. Our temporary refuge had been created out of the blue clay under the city decades ago. We must have been at or near the farthest terminus on the north side of the Chicago River.

I hesitated. The silence between the two of them deepened. I figured: better to try something sooner than later.

Baritone broke the silence abruptly. "You'd think those guys in the underground garage would have more than one stupid flashlight with crappy batteries. I hope they don't run out before the other guys get here. I don't want to wait in the darkness so they can jump us. Those two assholes are probably down here watching us. Why do we have to catch them, anyway? Let's just kill them and be done with it."

"Why don't you shut up?" Tenor asked.

Baritone grumbled a little more, but basically did as requested.

At this point, I figured out why the flashlight didn't move or waver. They'd placed it on a small outcropping halfway up the wall.

While Baritone had been talking, I began lowering myself to a squatting position and slowly began to run my hand along the floor, hunting for an article to toss beyond them to distract them. An old trick, but if it worked, I wasn't going to worry about being saved by the cliché.

I hoped Scott didn't try to squat as I was. His knees tended to pop liked cracked knuckles. The kind of noise from a mile away that would start a herd of buffalo stampeding, much less alert our two antagonists in this situation.

I found nothing in the immediate vicinity of my shoes. I raised my foot and took one careful duck-walk forward.

Scott tapped my shoulder and almost unbalanced me. I looked up at him, but I could barely make out the gleam of his eyes. He pointed back the way we had come. A pinprick of light glowed in the distance.

I fumbled more quickly for some object to throw. Scott tapped my shoulder again. I wanted to shout, "What?"

He pointed to his other hand. I moved my eyes close and saw the faint gleam of several coins. Obviously, our minds had thought along the same lines, only his worked a bit more logically than mine at the moment. I felt stupid for not thinking of checking my pockets, but grateful that he had.

I touched the front of my pants. I had my keys in one pocket and what felt like several quarters in another. I also had my wallet in my back pocket. It could serve if necessary.

I glanced back at the ever-growing light behind us, now the size of a half-dollar. If the guys ahead of us saw it, we'd be in trouble.

I unbent each body part as carefully and quickly as I could and stood up. Scott reared back his right arm to toss his handful of coins. I grabbed his hand to stop him. If he threw the whole handful, they could travel in random directions. It wouldn't do to have an object whiz by from our direction. I wanted the coin to land beyond them.

I held Scott's arm to keep him from throwing and took one of my coins. Carefully, I stretched my hand above my head. I touched the top of the tunnel before my arm was fully extended. I couldn't pitch them overhand. I lowered my arm to waist high, pulled it back, let it shoot forward, and heaved the coin sidearm down the tunnel.

The two men performed to perfection. They leaped up, grabbed the flashlight, and pointed it away from us, first down the tunnel we'd been traversing, then down the other.

"What the hell was that?" Baritone asked. "I don't like this! They're around here somewhere."

I could tell now that Tenor held the flashlight. He began to swing it back in our direction. Baritone raised a hand and fired down the tunnel where the sound had come from. The report echoed and thundered. We were still too far away to rush them under cover of the noise of the gunshot, but we crept forward slowly.

Tenor's hand with the flashlight swung back away from us. "Stop that!" he said. "Orders were no shooting. At least not yet."

"I'll defend myself," Baritone said.

When one of them had said, "Catch them" earlier, I thought perhaps they'd been told not to shoot. This new comment confirmed that possibility and gave me some comfort.

Baritone continued, "I'm not going to get caught. I'll kill them first."

"Shut up!" Tenor said.

I hoped they would keep talking to cover the sound of our approaching footfalls.

We were ten feet behind them when the figure with the flashlight looked back. "There's light behind us."

"The guys are coming," the deep voice said.

"Someone else is there," Tenor said.

"Now," I muttered. We rushed them.

Out of the corner of my eye, I saw Scott dive for the tenor and grab for the hand with the light. The beam wobbled and swung erratically. I jumped toward the hand with the gun which Baritone had begun to raise. My marine training proved to be not all for naught. I slammed his hand against the wall. A shot blasted the darkness. My ears rang. He still gripped the gun. I hoped the shots wouldn't cause a cave-in.

The tunnel behind us echoed with shouts. I wrapped both hands around Baritone's arm and tried to bang the wrist or fingers against the wall. He tried to bite me. I twisted around and managed to get an elbow under his jaw and knock him back a few feet. I'd spun around and was now facing back the way we'd come. At least three separate bright lights bobbed closer. Adrenaline poured into my body. I threw my whole weight behind smashing the hand with the gun against the wall.

Metal clacked against the cement. I got an arm loose and smashed the heel of my palm up against the bridge of his nose. He crumpled to the ground, and I heard whimpering in the baritone range.

I whirled to find Scott still locked in combat with Tenor. I grabbed the back of Tenor's hair and twisted and pulled back, then rammed his head nose first against the wall. He dropped the flashlight, met the floor, and stayed there.

Voices called behind us. I grabbed the gun off the floor, and Scott snatched up the flashlight.

Not much time to decide which tunnel. Scott leaped toward the opening leading to the intersecting passage and turned right, farther into the tunnel. He was moving, and I had no time to agree or disagree. No good to try going back. I followed him.

As my butt cleared the entrance, I heard shots ring out.

Into the ensuing silence, Baritone yelled, "Don't shoot! Don't shoot! You might hit us!"

A few precious seconds gained in the confusion and silence. Had the decision not to shoot been changed?

I didn't bother debating the safety of falling into a dead-fall, well, or cavern. We couldn't use the flashlight. It might light our way, but it would also make us great targets with them close behind.

"Run!" I yelled.

I felt—more than saw—the shadow of Scott's body speeding beside me. I heard the material on my shirt scrape against the wall as my arms pumped furiously. I glanced back once and saw a light flashing around a corner. I didn't slacken my pace, but I fired two rounds at random behind me. The two flashes from the gun gave a brief burst of light, but the roar of the firing made an incredible din. I didn't care whether I hit anything. I just wanted to scare them into not following—or at least hesitating, because now we were armed as well. It didn't work.

Out of the threatening darkness behind us a fusillade of bullets thundered and echoed through the tunnel. I dived into Scott, shoved him to the floor, and covered him with my body. Bullets rained for fifteen or twenty seconds. I felt a few faint bits of dust drift onto my cheek, from where a bullet must have hit in the ceiling above. My right arm and shoulder got soaked from a puddle of water.

"Are you hit?" I whispered in the echoing din.

"I'm okay," Scott muttered.

"We can't stay here," I said. "They'll simply come for us. We've got to run."

I heard his mumbled agreement.

"Now," I whispered.

We rose. I said, "Keep as close to the sides as you can." I didn't want to fire again because the tracings from my gunshots, I now realized, had shown them where to fire. As I ran, I tried rationalizing my not thinking about our being targets, but quickly gave it up amid the desire to keep air flowing into my lungs, and the growing fear that I would plow into something, or trip and break a vital limb leaving myself to the mercy of whoever had killed Glen.

I turned my head back for a second. No lights behind us. Maybe at least one of them had figured out that their lights presented a target for us to shoot at, as well.

Down the tunnel we fled, reckless in our fear. Our narrow confines allowed the sounds of pursuit from behind to echo and reecho, making it seem, at times, as if our hunters were inches behind us.

Suddenly the tunnel began to slope down. Then lack of wall touching my elbow and a sense of spaciousness on either side made me aware that we were at a junction.

I reached out for Scott.

"Which way?" he whispered. His words seemed as loud as the last trumpet on Judgment Day.

If I remembered the general idea of the tunnels from all

the flood stories, they moved generally west and south from where we were. If we had been traveling south, then we certainly didn't want to take the left-hand opening, which would lead toward the lake. The tunnels dead-ended or turned back upon themselves before reaching Lake Michigan.

Not a lot of time to choose.

"Right," I said. "At least we'll be out of any line of fire if they decide to start shooting again."

"What if that tunnel that was paralleling ours comes out near here?" Scott asked. "Some of them could have followed it and used lights. They could have leapfrogged ahead of us and be to our right."

"Then straight ahead. No more time to argue. Let's move."

The sounds of pursuit grew fainter, so we employed more care now as we rushed forward. The tunnel floor continued to slope downward, apparently for the trip under the river.

Visions of tons of water breaking through and trapping and drowning us popped into my head. Supposedly the city was making more inspections and bulkheads were being installed to prevent another flood like last time. Which brought another unbidden thought: What if they already had installed the bulkheads along here, and we were rushing headlong into a trap no matter which branching we took? At least now I had a gun. Maybe we could hole up in some obscure cranny. Probably couldn't hold out long. No one knew where we were. I didn't know how often they inspected, or whether the workers on the bulkheads put in overtime on weekends.

We came to another crossing and hesitated, then whirled around uncertainly. I listened for a few moments. Not even an echo pursued us. Maybe we were outdistancing them. I put my arm out to point forward and touched metal. Another couple of steps, and we'd have run into a bulkhead. To the left was the lake. We took the right-hand turn.

The aroma of a cat-litter box had been slowly turning into that of a monkey house which desperately needed cleaning. Now that stench of unwashed cages began to overpower us.

"I think we'd better try the light," Scott said.

"It's not too dangerous?" I asked.

"Whatever is making that stink is more dangerous than what's behind us. Listen," he said.

Silence impenetrable fell. I strained to listen. Then I caught a light skittering, screechy noise.

Scott switched on the light. At first we couldn't see anything, but we walked forward slowly. Another fifty feet, and at the far edge of the glow from the light, I thought I caught a glimpse of a moving carpet of gray. We stopped. Hundreds, maybe thousands of verminous creatures barred our way.

I stifled my impulse to turn and run.

Scott played the light along the walls. We could see a faint crack through which the animals seemed to move. About forty feet farther along was another junction.

"Will they attack us?" I asked.

"Not if we keep moving."

"We aren't going to try and walk through them?"

"No, but we can't go back. Let's try for that junction."

Going back was useless. Going close to rats was our only hope. We began inching forward.

"We haven't met many so far," I murmured.

"I think all the boarding up of exits has taken away their food supply. They won't stay anyplace that has no food."

We proceeded at a slow, steady pace.

"I think they're frightened of the light," Scott said.

Perhaps it was my imagination or the dimness or the fall of the light that made these critters seem to be the size of the proverbial Toyota. I knew this wasn't the environment in which either of us wanted to meet the vermin elite.

We turned the corner we'd seen and moved away from the rats. I felt a shiver through my body when we finally turned off the light. We had to save the battery. Slowly the smell became less overpowering. After a while, I put the gun in my belt.

I could hear Scott and touch him, but I desperately wanted to see him. His facial expressions as he talked. The cleft of his chin, the gleam in his eyes when he was about to make me laugh, his broad shoulders, the tiny cone-shaped mole just below his butt on his left leg.

We strode forward while holding out our hands in front of our bodies. An eerie length of time later, I touched solid metal on my right.

"Turn on the flashlight," I said.

Scott whirled the beam around and caught a shadow to the left. I moved up to examine it.

Metal rungs. Narrow and rusted. He played the beam upward. The glorious steps led into darkness, but it was up, not forward. I leaped toward the bottom rung. I bumped against Scott. The flashlight fell and winked out. I tried to grab it, missed the step, and sprawled forward, banging my head on the cement.

"You okay?" Scott called.

Moments later, I felt his hands touching my left arm.

"I'm fine," I said.

I tapped my hand on the ground to find the flashlight. I could feel Scott next to me doing the same.

"Got it," he said a minute later.

"Turn it on!" I ordered.

"I'm trying to. I think it's broken."

I felt stupid for screwing up, and now giving commands. Of course he would try to turn it on.

When the light didn't reappear immediately, I got truly frightened.

"It's not going to work," I said. "It's my fault. I'm sorry."

"Forget it."

I heard the clunk of metal on cement and then the roll of the flashlight.

"Did you throw it away?" I asked.

"It's broken," Scott said. "We can't fix it."

I was torn between yelling at him for flinging it away and feelings of guilt for causing him to drop it in the first place.

"Let's try to find the rungs," Scott said.

We stepped close to each other and then began moving to the sides, touching every inch of wall.

I didn't say anything about if this way was blocked above, that we should have kept the flashlight and maybe tried to fix it. How would we anyway, in total darkness?

I groped along the wall for a few minutes. Suddenly my hand touched metal. I called to Scott. When I felt him next to me, I reached for his hand and brought it to the metal.

"I'll climb first," I said. "Probably be good if you stick right behind me."

"Yeah," he said.

I had seen a narrow railing on each side before he dropped the light. Now I clutched each of these and began my ascent.

Several times the stairs turned through narrow openings, but up I climbed, listening to Scott moving below me.

After maybe thirty steps I saw it. "Light ahead!" I shouted. It didn't seem like daylight and it was faint, but in that darkness it might as well have been the blaze of the sun. Maybe twenty more steps, and I could see that the light came from various pinprick-sized holes in a round object. Dim as it was, at least I could see.

"It's like some kind of manhole cover," I announced to Scott when I arrived near the top. The steps continued to the covering. I grabbed hold of one railing with my left hand and banged the other against the manhole. It didn't budge.

I could see that the opening we were in was big enough for three people to stand next to each other in, if there had been a floor.

"What's wrong?" Scott asked.

"It won't move," I said. I examined the blockage carefully. Two hinges held the left side of the cover, but I couldn't find any other protuberances. The lock would be on the side away from us. I pulled the gun out of my belt.

"You're not going to shoot!" Scott said.

I turned the gun around and held it by the barrel. "No," I said as I began banging away at the pins holding a hinge. I knew the sound of the gun being fired in this narrow place would deafen us, perhaps leaving permanent damage.

I tapped at it vigorously, but it wouldn't budge. I gripped the railing carefully with one hand, planted one foot on the rung, and found a hold for the other on the opposite wall. I swung hard. Nothing. I summoned a reserve of strength and whammed it. A quarter-inch movement, but enough for a huge surge of hope. A few minutes' work, and it was gone. The second proved even more recalcitrant, but with a last swing, the gun butt cracked, and the pin flew into the darkness below.

I shoved at the lid. It scraped open. I clambered up and onto a floor, turned around, knelt down, and gave Scott a hand up.

We were inside a small room. The light came from an opaque fixture which glowed yellow above a sign that said "Danger. Wear Your Hard Hat."

By the light, I could see mounds of thick cables connected to banks of switches on all the walls. I took a step toward the door. It flew open. Framed against the blackness of night was a well-fed man who said, "What the hell are you doing here?"

Turned out we were in the middle of an electrical substation a few feet north of and under the Merchandise Mart. We explained everything twice to him, then to several electric-company officials, and finally to the police.

Most of them instantly recognized Scott Carpenter, the baseball player. You win more than a few World Series games and make millions a year, people in Chicago will take notice. They barely took notice of me as Tom Mason, non-famous person. At this moment, their recognition of him and the goodwill it brought were very good things.

Somebody asked whether we wanted food. We said no. It was a little after five in the morning.

Our news about a murder at Scott's place kept any fawning and good fellowship on the part of the police to a minimum.

We rode to the penthouse in the back of an unmarked cop car. Numerous other police joined us in the lobby of Scott's building.

Howard wasn't on duty. The morning guard told us that she hadn't seen anything strange, and that when she took over, Howard had acted normal.

The cops, led by a slender detective, maybe in his mid-forties, with a hatchet face and a long nose, whose name was Joe Quinn, insisted that we give them the key and that they go up ahead of us. Two plainclothes cops and two uniforms took the journey to the penthouse.

Fifteen minutes later, the two detectives came down with strange looks on their faces. "Are you guys shitting us?" Quinn asked.

"What's wrong?" I asked.

He crooked his finger at us to follow him. We gathered on the elevator. As we rode up, I asked, "What's going on?"

"You're going to tell us."

"We didn't kill him," Scott said.

Quinn said nothing.

At the door the uniformed officer gave us an odd look. We hurried inside.

The body was gone.

We rushed over to the windows. Only a small rust-colored stain remained to mark the spot of Glen Proctor's demise.

Scott and I gaped at each other, then turned to face the police.

"He was here," Scott said. "I swear to God."

Something truly outré had happened, and I was angry, but a granite mass of fear rested at the pit of my stomach.

I knelt down and felt the rug. It was slightly damp. "This could be his blood," I said.

"Or not," Quinn said.

"Why would we make this up?" Scott asked.

"I don't know," Quinn said. "Maybe you could tell us. We don't need this kind of shit. We've got plenty of real cases to deal with, not this crap."

"Look," I said. "We didn't make it up. There was a dead guy here. Glen Proctor, the baseball player. He just got in from Mexico. You could call down there to the team or check the airlines. He came here. Call his parents' house. They live in the area. Check with Howard, the night security man. He might have seen the guys who were after us."

Quinn growled. Jess Bolewski, his partner, a guy with thinning hair that he combed straight back in lonely strands, said, "We could make a couple of calls. You better hope some part of this checks out."

"His luggage is in the bedroom," I said. "I'll show you." Bolewski followed me down the hall to the room Proctor had been staying in. All of his things were gone. The room looked as if a cleaning service had been through it. I checked the bathroom he'd been using. Totally spotless.

"Why are you guys doing this?" the cop asked.

"We aren't doing anything," I said. "It really happened. I saw it. I touched him."

Back in the living room, Quinn was on the phone. I listened to his half of the conversation. "We got no dead body . . . I don't know yet . . . Don't strike me as the hysterical type . . . We'll get to the bottom of it." He hung up.

"No luggage," Bolewski told his partner.

I was angry, confused, and frightened. "The ability to

move that quickly and cover their tracks means it's a big-time outfit," I said.

Bolewski said, "You're saying that some nasty people killed him, left, then said, 'Oh, gosh, let's not leave our mess to clean up,' and hurried back here to neaten the place?"

"No!" I snapped.

A few moments' silence passed before Quinn asked, "Anybody else see Proctor here?"

We shook our heads. He'd gotten in late Friday. Scott said he hadn't gone out or called anyone.

"At least make the calls I suggested," I said. "We have no reason to lie to you."

Quinn agreed to try calling. We sat on the white leather couches in the living room.

"What airline?" Quinn asked.

"He told us he flew Air Mexico," Scott said.

The detective called the airline, identified himself, and told the person on the other end what he needed. From what he said, I gathered he was being put through to a supervisor. Quinn turned to his buddy and said, "Tough finding somebody to give me information this early in the morning."

Eventually he was connected. The significant part came when he said, "No record. You're sure?" He listened a minute more, thanked the person, and then turned to us.

"You sure he was on Air Mexico?" Quinn asked.

"That's what he told us," Scott said.

"They have no record of him being on any plane, and to take an international flight you have to show your pass-port. Are you saying he had a fake passport?"

"I don't know," I said. "We're just telling you what he told us. Can't you check the other airlines?"

"Yeah, but it'll take a while. Why would this guy lie to you?" Quinn asked.

"He told us he was in trouble," I said.

"What kind of trouble?" the cop asked.

"He didn't say."

"You let him stay here without knowing what was going on?"

"He was a friend," Scott said. "He told me he'd explain, but that he just needed a place to stay and could we put him up? He's a good friend. I trusted him."

"Isn't he the baseball player that's been suspended for drugs?" Bolewski asked.

"Yes," I said.

Quinn made another call. "I need the number for Proctor either in 708 or 312 area code," he said into the receiver. "The real estate guy—try the North Shore first."

He jotted a few numbers on paper in his regulation blue notebook. He punched in the number. He had to wait some time for an answer. He stood up and trailing the forty-foot cord, paced the length of the room in front of the floor-to-ceiling windows.

When someone answered, he stopped walking. Quinn identified himself and asked for Mr. Proctor. After a lengthy pause, he again identified himself, then asked if Glen Proctor was there or if they knew where he was.

Several minutes of conversation followed. When he was finished, Quinn came back and sat across from us. "They haven't heard from him," he said. "As far as they know, he's in Mexico getting ready for or making contacts for winter baseball. He is supposed to be doing some traveling down there at the moment. He could be anywhere in the country. We could call the team tomorrow and see if they've seen him or have any guess as to where he might be. Confirming his whereabouts won't be easy."

Interviewing Howard the security man necessitated rousting building management and more lengthy explanations. But after a final phone call, Quinn said, "He didn't see a thing out of the ordinary."

"One too many naps, or they got to him," Scott said.

"Glen Proctor was here," I said. "He had two bullet holes in him. One was—"

Quinn cut me off. "What do you want us to do? Say we buy your story. What could we do? We don't have a corpse. Tough to prove a murder without a body. Okay, you saw it, but where is it? You don't just tootle around the city with a dead body draped over your shoulder."

"The guys who work in the parking garage," I said. "They must have seen something."

Quinn directed one of the uniformed cops to go downstairs and check it out.

"Can't you guys get the crime lab up here?" Scott said. "You could take fibers from the carpet. That stain has to prove something."

"The crime lab, when there isn't a crime?" Bolewski made it sound as if we were really dumb and that he was getting truly fed up.

"The crime lab comes," Quinn said. "They take samples. Say they find blood. Who's to say it isn't yours or somebody else's? Do you know Proctor's blood type? If they found fibers from a jacket or piece of clothing, we have only your word that's what Proctor was wearing. If they could track the DNA of what they found, what do you have from Proctor that would show it was his?"

"And if we do find evidence," Bolewski said, "what's to keep us from thinking either one or both of you killed him?"

I thought escaping from the tunnels would be our biggest problem.

The cop returned from downstairs. "The guy who was working the parking garage went home after his shift. I called him from downstairs. He says the only thing that happened was after three this morning, when a couple guys in gray suits came in, said they were waiting for one of the tenants. The attendant said he had to park a few cars. When he came back they were gone, and he didn't see them again. Says he didn't see or hear anything suspicious, and no, he wouldn't recognize them again."

Bolewski glared at us.

Quinn said, "Why don't you guys really tell us what this is all about?"

Both Scott and I used every argument we could think of to try and convince them.

At one point Quinn said, "It would be a lot easier if you could give us anything tangible to prove your point."

Both of us spoke passionately in a desperate attempt to be believed. We even followed the cops down in the elevator as they left trying to get in a few more words that would tip the scale to get them to believe us.

Bolewski didn't even want to listen, and he made it evident with elaborate sounds of disgust every time one of us would try to make a telling point.

Outside, Bolewski immediately hopped into the car. Quinn said, "I promise to do a little checking. This is too screwy. I want to believe you guys."

Quinn got in the car, and they drove off. One of the uniformed cops edged up to Scott and held out a little notepad. He asked Scott for an autograph for his kid. Almost reflexively Scott reached out his hand for the pen.

I gave a disgusted sigh.

3

Sweeping down the street from the north through the mist was Lester Smitherton walking his two German shepherds. The dogs heeled one to each side while Lester held the leashes in limp wrists. He wore a shocking-pink jacket almost brighter than the sun rising about us. He wore fluffy blue warm-up pants appliquéd with pink lightning bolts. He wore bright white tennis shoes with tiny pink dots on them. He loved to wear this or even more outrageous outfits when he walked the dogs. He often expressed the desire for gay-bashers to try and mug him while he was in the company of Oscar and Wilde. He'd had them specially trained to defend him.

I'd met Lester ten years ago in a used-record shop up in Rogers Park. We'd been hunting through the folk-music bin. I'd been there first and picked up a long-out-of-print Bob Gibson album.

His first words to me were "I'll give you fifty dollars for that album."

We'd wound up having a long discussion about collecting folk music. I was really just an amateur, trying to find artists I liked. Lester was an eclectic connoisseur, concentrating not only on folk music but on a wide variety of esoterica. One of his most prized finds was a ten-inch album by Blossom Dearie from the 1950s made by WVBR in Ithaca, New York. He also collected popular music of the forties and fifties, especially Jo Stafford, whom I also liked. His absolute favorites, which he insisted on showing everyone who entered his home, were something I thought made him wonderfully unique. He had a collection of original albums with teen tragedy songs on them from the late fifties and early sixties. He loved nothing better than a group wailing a pathetically schmaltzy simple melody of hopeless love.

He never played any of the records but once, that to record them on tape—and then he made a tape of the tape to store in a safe-deposit box.

We'd gone out for coffee that first day. Afterward, we'd kept up contact. Lester had invited us to a few parties and, over the years, the three of us had become good friends. Occasionally he gave investment tips to Scott, who passed them on to his accountant. Several had paid big dividends.

He lived in one of the few mansions still standing on Lake Shore Drive north of Oak Street just a block and a half from our place. His investments had been shrewd and immensely profitable. He was an investment banker in one of the big La Salle Street firms and had been for twenty years. He'd also inherited a substantial pile when a favorite uncle died.

As he approached us, the dogs began to wag their tails. Lester smiled and waved. When Lester stopped three feet from us, the dogs immediately sat down.

"What's wrong?" Lester asked us.

"I don't believe it," I said.

"You both look exhausted. I'm about to make breakfast. You must come to my place and let me fix you something." Lester was also a master chef.

Although I hadn't slept, I found that my nerves were still strung far too taut for me to fall asleep. I agreed.

"That sounds good," Scott said.

We walked the short distance to Lester's. First he served us exquisite coffee in the living room. One dog sat on either side of Lester's chair. The living room was what one of his ex-lovers had called the trash room. Lester had the money to indulge his whimsical tastes. All those little knickknacks you almost impulsively bought, but came to your senses in time—Lester had them in this room. In addition he attended conventions where thrift shops could purchase mounds of useless merchandise. This room was a trash nightmare. Among other things scattered along the shelves were a Dutch civil-defense urinal, a music box that played a funeral march, round plugs of Astroturf left over from the manufacture of putting greens, and a collection of parachute rings. This was not to mention the more mainstream debris of a 3-D View Master from the 1950s, a hubcap from a 1947 Studebaker, a Don King troll doll, and a glass case filled with his belt-buckle collection.

Lester was in his fifties with short grizzled hair, a deep cleft in his chin, and a slender although unmuscular body. He settled himself in his favorite canary-yellow overstuffed chair, drew his knees up to his chest, wrapped his arms around them, and said, "Tell me all."

I explained everything to him. When I finished, I summed up. "Somebody killed Glen Proctor. We got chased, but not shot at as aggressively as we could have been. Someone broke in and took the body away from the penthouse. These people got by security twice."

Lester said, "While I make breakfast, we must think of a plan."

I discovered I was ravenous. The night before, at the fund-raiser, we had dined on that peculiar form of dead chicken grown, I was sure, for just such banquets. The tasteless, dried-out bird that gives its life so you'll open your wallet and give your money.

I generally didn't like being in Lester's kitchen. I hate to cook, and you could barely look anywhere in this kitchen without observing clues that a gourmet lurked nearby. On the top of a set of cabinets and hanging on a wall was a vast collection of all the modern cooking gadgets sold at all the trendier stores. The only ones I remotely recognized were the graduated wire whisks, whose function I could never understand. One simple fork did most of the mixing I needed.

Dangling from the ceiling were enough copper pots to obscure half the ceiling. What was worse, Lester knew how to use every device in the kitchen and loved to entertain with lavish dinners for small, intimate groups of friends.

Lester began yanking vegetables out of the refrigerator and placing them on the butcher-block table in the center of the room. "I know a Jason Proctor," Lester said. "Filthy rich."

"Same family," Scott said. "Remember the time I got you passes to the field before the game?"

Lester nodded.

"Glen Proctor was the one horsing around with the baseball bat."

"The one rubbing it up the butt crack of the dark-haired outfielder?" Lester's eyes shone.

"Him," Scott said.

"Is he . . . ?"

"No," Scott said.

"A practical-joke-playing, straight prick tease," I said.

"He was very blond and sexy, like Scott," Lester said.

"Was not," I said.

Lester ignored us and asked, "Why are you in peril? You were not in jeopardy before Proctor came. You are now. Therefore, and quite obviously, you are in danger because of Proctor. What have you done?"

"We let him stay at our place," Scott said.

"Not something to kill somebody for," Lester said.

"It's not as if we were protecting or hiding him," I said. "We didn't think it was some kind of secret."

"Nor, evidently, was it a secret to whoever is bothering you," Lester said. "They killed him. Leaving aside their reasons for doing him in, what makes it necessary to do you two?"

"We know something," I said. "Or Proctor brought something into the penthouse that they want?"

"Why not just take what they want and leave you alone?" Lester asked.

"We'd be happy to give it to them, if we knew what it was," Scott said.

"Did either of you see the contents of his luggage?" Lester asked.

I said, "I didn't see anything except him strutting around in his blue jeans, starched white shirt, and gym socks the first night, or yesterday prancing around in his underwear and then in a pair of the skimpiest gym shorts I've ever seen."

While we talked, Lester's hands flew as he diced vegetables, whisked eggs, shook out spices, and sliced fresh bread.

Scott said, "I helped him carry his stuff in. I didn't see anything unusual. When I got up early to go to the bathroom yesterday morning, I ran into him. We sat in the breakfast nook for about an hour and talked before Tom got up."

"Why didn't you tell me this?" I demanded.

"I don't report all my conversations to you," Scott said.

"Did he tell you anything that might explain what's been going on?" The cold asperity in my voice matched the angry annoyance in his.

Scott glared at me, then said, "He told me nothing I can think of connected to all this. Do you think I wouldn't have told you if he'd said something that could help us?"

My good sense told me he would have, but the angry and frightened part of me wanted to throttle him for not telling me about their conversation.

"Gentlemen," Lester said. "We need to stick to the questions at hand. One major concern is, did you see anything Proctor had that might have some value?"

Scott shook his head.

"He gave us presents," I said. I explained about the necklaces Proctor had given us.

Scott unhooked the chain and handed it to Lester, who ran a critical eye over it.

"I have no idea whether these are real," he said. "From what you say about him and his so-called deals that have turned out to be duds, I have my doubts. Although this is the most beautiful green." He shook his head and handed it back to Scott. "Either he got taken, or he wanted to impress you with a little glitter and glass. These could be the crown jewels of King Otho the Insignificant or a national treasure of Mexico smuggled out of the country."

"We've got to use logic and common sense," I said. "Maybe it's really simple. You constantly see headlines about drugs flooding in from Mexico, South America, and the Caribbean. This could easily be some kind of drug deal gone bad. Proctor has the reputation. Maybe he found the opportunity."

"We never saw any drugs," Scott said. "He certainly never mentioned it, but his suitcases were gone; so if he had any on him, whoever was after him took it with them."

"He wouldn't necessarily mention it to you, if he was trying to use you in some way," Lester suggested.

"Use us how?" I asked.

Lester shrugged. "I don't know. What I think is essential to figure out is, if they got what they wanted, why keep after you?"

"Proctor said he came straight to our place from the airport," Scott said. "We have no proof of that. Maybe he took the stuff and hid it someplace in the city. Could be whoever is after us thinks we know where it is."

"If they are still looking for something, then it would make sense to keep us alive," I said.

"If they found it without the information they think you have, why waste the time to come back and kill you?" Lester asked.

"I don't know," I answered.

"Did they ransack your place?" Lester asked.

"No," I said.

"Then maybe they weren't looking for something."

"Then why take the luggage?" I asked.

"Was it gone the first time you came back?" Lester asked.

"I don't know. We didn't have time to look in the bedroom."

"So they could have killed him for the luggage or come back for him and the luggage."

"That's what I don't get," Scott said. "Why come back for him? They must have known we'd report it to the police."

"Not if they made you dead first," Lester said.

"But they didn't stay and wait for us to come home to kill us," Scott said.

Lester rubbed his hands together with all-too-much eagerness. "What a wonderful series of puzzles!" he said.

I ignored my annoyance at his delight. "We've got to sort this out, or we could get killed," I said. "They weren't looking for something, but they took the luggage. Proctor is dead, but they come back, and then take the body to make it look like nothing happened. That defies logic."

"Not to the people who did it," Lester said.

"They didn't want a particular thing the second time," Scott said. "They wanted us. We didn't get shot at until we were in the tunnels. Maybe because they'd ordered us to be taken alive, but then why start shooting?"

"It's crazy," Lester commented.

"We knew or know something," I said.

"Or they think you do," Lester added.

"A secret that Proctor was supposed to tell us?" Scott said.

"But what did he tell us? Except for the conversation you had with him this morning, we were both around when he talked. I didn't hear him say anything that somebody might kill him for."

"He didn't say anything to me," Scott said. "He mostly

talked about baseball, or how proud he was to be free of drugs and alcohol, and how he was sure he'd make a contribution to his team next year."

"You're sure?" I asked.

"Yes," Scott said.

Silence permeated the room for several minutes while Lester set a magnificent repast before us.

After slaking my appetite, I said, "I'd like to talk to the Proctor family. They have a right to know what's happened to their son. Also, they've got to have some idea of what's going on."

Lester said, "I have some connection with Mr. Proctor from my work at the bank. We aren't best friends, but we play a round of golf once in a while. I had a hand in a few of his deals. I may be able to get you in to talk to him."

"You golf and you're gay," I said. "You must be the only gay person on the planet who plays golf."

"I forced myself to learn," Lester said. "My straight clients get so impressed if I can golf."

"What kind of guy is Mr. Proctor?" Scott asked.

"Fiercely aggressive," Lester said. "Hates to lose at golf or anything else. Big in real estate in this city. If he's not the biggest, he's pretty damn close to the top. Buys and sells huge or expensive or both pieces of property. Makes enormous profits. Lots of battles over the years. Can't stand to lose."

"How can you deal with that kind of person?" Scott asked.

"Business," Lester answered. "You want to do deals in this town, you'll bump up against old man Proctor at some point. I'm surprised you'd be bothered by fierce competition. I've seen you pitch. It's a battle, and the most warlike wins."

"Not like that," Scott said. "We're paid to entertain and supposedly win. The owners may be rapacious monsters, but for most players it's a job."

"That's what this is for Proctor—his job—and he's very good at it."

As we finished the meal, Lester promised to do what he could to get us in to see Jason Proctor.

I prodded Lester to tell us more about the Proctor family finances.

"Wealth, wealth, and more wealth. Orrin Proctor, the grandfather of young Glen, owned several railroads. He invested in Canadian municipal bonds and gold just before the stock market crash in 1929, so he was spared its horrors. He managed to hold onto and eventually increase his wealth. Jason Proctor, immediate sire of Glen, could have lived a life of luxury simply on what Daddy had, but Jason had ambitions. He began to branch out and dabble in many fields. Always seemed to make a go of them. He invested in two movies, and they became blockbusters. Threw money into Texas oil in the early eighties, and then ran just before the crash came in the mid-eighties. He's had a lot of luck."

"Where does most of his money come from now?" I asked.

"Investments in just about anything," Lester said. "A guy with that much wealth has his finger in a zillion pies. Shopping centers in Singapore, an office building in Zurich, an auto-parts monopoly in Santiago, Chile, and hundreds of things in between."

"Is he a billionaire?" I asked.

"Not quite that much, but enough so he could retire today and live for the rest of his life in luxury unknown to most of the inhabitants of the globe."

"Do you know anything about Glen's mother?" I asked.

"I have never met Mrs. Proctor. She is in real estate also. Rumored and real marital problems have plagued them both for years. She is supposedly at least as rich as he in her own right. They'd break any law to get back at each other. When you're that rich, you can ignore most codes of conduct. You become a law unto yourself. I've dealt with him, but not her. If you'd like, I can try and get more information about both of them for you."

I told him I'd appreciate it if he would.

A few minutes later, we thanked Lester for breakfast and left. We trudged in silence back up the Inner Drive. I found I was exhausted. It was after nine in the morning. At this hour on Sunday, the Inner Drive was crowded with shoppers heading for breakfast, brunch, or the stores on North Michigan Avenue. On the Inner Drive, which passed immediately in front of our building, a line of honking cars crept around a stopped carriage. Chicago has those ubiquitous carriage rides that clop people around the streets at a pace guaranteed to blow at least a few drivers' tempers, although the time Scott and I took one in San Francisco, it had been reasonably pleasant and romantic.

This one was stopped because the driver was arguing with the passengers. They wanted to get out now. I couldn't help hearing the shouted arguments.

As we neared our door, I began to wonder about our safety. If they'd attacked once, why not again? I didn't think we were in the clear yet. We'd have to find a place to take refuge.

Across the way, the couple in the carriage were now arguing with each other. In voices that could be heard at least a block away, each was accusing the other of making a public spectacle. The gist of the whole thing seemed to be that the man wanted a full refund and the woman wanted to go home. So much for romance. The driver intermittently added an antiphon to their duet. Mostly he wanted his money.

Finally the woman leaped from the carriage and began stalking away. Her date climbed down but seemed torn between following her and getting his money. He and the driver continued a discussion in a more modulated range.

Scott pointed to the carriage and said, "The whole world has gone crazy."

"I wanted to lose my temper with those cops," I said.

"I was close a couple times, but it's probably better we didn't. Quinn sort of sounded like he was willing to listen."

"I hated Bolewski," I said.

We were talking outside our building. Scott rubbed his arms. We hadn't worn our jackets, and it was cool.

"What happened to Glen and why?" I asked. "How can we prove it? How can we get something the cops will believe?"

"They'll track the team down in Mexico," Scott said. "They can try to confirm whether he was there or not."

"But it won't prove he had two bullet holes in him on our living-room floor."

"It's a start."

I turned toward the door. Two men in gray suits emerged from around a dark corner on the north side of the building. I grabbed Scott.

"What?" he said. He turned to look.

I swiveled my head around. Two more men, both with guns out, were approaching from the south end of the building. I twisted my head back. The first two now flashed some lethal-looking artillery. All four seemed to be in decent-enough shape to give us a good chase if we tried to run, although they had us boxed fairly well right and left and flight in those directions was cut off.

In seconds, I was pulling Scott after me to the only alternative.

We dashed toward Lake Shore Drive. I was willing to cause a multi-car pile-up if it would draw attention to our plight. First we dove out onto the Inner Drive. To the left I saw a row of southbound cars rushing toward us. They had just been released from the stoplight at La Salle Drive. We made it across ahead of them. Our pursuers were stuck behind this vehicular barrier.

Two shots rang out as I eased around one of the cars maneuvering slowly past the carriage. The passenger was just handing the driver some money. They both gaped at us.

I crouched behind the carriage. Scott joined me as several more shots rang out. The passenger took off running. The driver looked from us to the guys attempting to dodge the traffic. Another shot rang out, striking the pavement inches from my left hand. The driver chose discretion and bolted. The horse whinnied, flicked its ears, and tried to pull the carriage with it. For the moment the animal's being used to the noise and chaos of the city and the brake being in place, kept the horse from going berserk.

I didn't want to leave the temporary safety of the carriage. I was still willing to try a dash across the Drive, but their shooting added a dangerous dimension.

I wondered why hadn't they shot at us immediately, earlier, when it had been much less public?

Scott said, "Follow me."

He leaped into the carriage and grabbed the reins. I tumbled in after him. He ducked down as well as he could, released the brake and flicked the whip at the old nag. The carriage lurched forward as more shots rang out.

For a minute, we trotted down the road. I kept my head down. Scott knelt on the carriage floor with legs spraddled, urging the horse to greater swiftness. Balancing myself with both hands I eased my head up so that my eyes peeked over the bunting around the backseat. A stream of cars followed us, the ones on the left passing, with the occupants staring at us.

Two guys, waving their guns and running furiously, chased us on foot. I saw a car start up on the side street next to our building. The car's tires screeched and the vehicle headed north into the temporarily vacant southbound lanes and came barreling after us. I looked forward. Another set of cars, released from La Salle Drive, approached rapidly.

We were about two hundred yards from the corner ourselves when I glanced behind. One of the gunmen stopped

50

running and aimed carefully. With the rapidly expanding distance and the violent shaking of the carriage, I doubted whether he could hit us, but I grabbed Scott and made him duck. I heard several shots but didn't notice that anything hit us. When I looked again, one hood had resumed the chase and was falling farther behind. The other was re-loading.

The poor old mare had long since passed from a trot to a dead run. By this time the carriage was careening nearly out of control.

Brakes squealed behind us as our pursuers met the on-coming traffic. My head bobbed with the motion of the carriage as I watched the pursuing car face the onslaught. Horns blared as the driver wrenched the vehicle into the northbound lanes.

I looked ahead. Scott now stood up with his legs spread wide, hips against the rim of the carriage, balancing him-self against the wild swaying of our escape vehicle. With the reins gathered in one hand, and the whip flicking out over the back of the horse in the other, he looked just like a Roman charioteer. I'd have loved to be in a chariot race if this is what it would have been like, but more practical considerations quickly overcame the thrill of a dash remi-niscent of ages past.

"Get down!" I shouted.

I swear to God, he actually yelled, "Yee-ha!" and then cracked the whip over the horse's back. His only response to my warning was to bend his knees slightly. He glanced back, flicked the reins, employed the whip, turned forward again, and gave another yell. We rushed on.

I examined the activity at the intersection ahead. Cars streamed by on La Salle Drive moving to or from Lake Shore Drive. Traffic continued to flow heavily. La Salle Drive was one of the major entrances to the Drive for people who'd spent some time on the Near North Side of Chicago enjoying the plethora of shops and restaurants available.

As we neared the light, it changed to red in our direction. Scott swung out into the emptying southbound lanes and maneuvered into the intersection. The cars starting up from our left and right stopped abruptly. Horns blared, but we raced across La Salle. Once again, our pursuers jumped into the southbound lane, but they were too far behind and, after we passed, the traffic flowed forward from both directions. Our attackers ran up against a wall of moving protective autos. I heard the crunch of metal on metal.

I looked back. They'd tried to force themselves through the traffic. I hoped they'd had a multi-vehicle, traffic-snarling accident.

Scott didn't spend much time on La Salle Drive. Within seconds, we were on the grassy area of Lincoln Park, moving rapidly north and west toward the zoo.

I stood up facing backward and felt the racing wind on my back. I could see brake lights still jammed together at the intersection, but we were too far away for me to pick out the car that had been chasing us.

I turned back to Scott.

"This horse isn't going to be able to keep this up much longer," he said. "She's old, and I'm sure she hasn't gone this fast in a long time."

"We've got to find someplace to hide and call the cops. They have to believe us now."

"They'll believe the gunshots," Scott said. The horse had slowed to a trot. "Into the zoo?"

"No. I don't know my way around."

Lincoln Park Zoo was the most-often-visited zoo in the country and one of the few that was still free. I hadn't been since my parents took me when I was five. I barely remembered it. I didn't want to be driving a horse and carriage around aimlessly in an unfamiliar environment.

"We'll leave the horse and carriage in the park. If they find it, they'll have to guess whether we're in the zoo or back into the neighborhoods."

Scott drove about half a block past the exit to Dickens

Street. He tied the horse to a tree on the east side of the road. Ducking behind cars and keeping to shadows, we raced back.

Seeing no traffic on Dickens or Marine Drive we ran west. At Clark Street we stood in a shadow until all traffic had passed. Of course, we didn't see a cop car. We burst across the street and tore down the block toward Lincoln Avenue.

A car turned from Hudson Street onto Dickens and began to cruise slowly toward us. I shoved Scott into a shadowed doorway. We froze while the car passed. It turned out to be a Toyota Tercel with two women in the front seat. So far I hadn't noted any of our nemeses being women.

"Where the hell are we running to?" Scott asked.

I drew deep breaths. "Call the cops?"

"I don't see a phone booth. Can we afford to be in one spot for too long?"

"No." I glanced both ways down the street. No cars were coming. "Maybe we can get a cab on Lincoln Avenue."

We dashed west on Dickens to the corner. For the moment, Lincoln Avenue was devoid of traffic.

"We can't stay out in the open like this," Scott said.

We ran west and at Oz Park cut across it toward the northwest. At the corner of Webster and Halsted, we stopped for a second.

"Traffic coming from both ways," Scott said.

Quickly I looked for a place of refuge. A doorway loomed several feet away. "There," I said and ran in. I opened the door. We stumbled down several stairs but landed standing in the middle of a tile-covered lobby. Each of three walls had one couch with ripped dark-red vinyl cushions. The fourth wall had a reception desk.

No one stood at the desk, but I heard cheerful humming coming from somewhere farther inside. I glanced out the windows that you had to look up to see out of from the sunken lobby. I thought I saw a dark sedan like the one that had been chasing us. I slunk across the lobby and tried the door that I assumed led to the rooms. It was locked.

I ran up to the counter of the reception desk and banged the little bell. It gave off a tiny ching. The humming stopped. A perfectly immense woman emerged from behind a six-foot switchboard.

She eyed us carefully. "You look like hell," she stated. She leaned her bulk against the counter from the other side. She could easily have wrapped us both in her fond embrace and had room for one more. Her gray hair was pulled straight back, but left to dangle in wisps of curls at her neck. The color of her eyes was lost behind thick glasses, through which she inspected both of us in turn.

"I'm Edna," she said. "I own the hotel. You boys look like you need some help."

I didn't want to make long explanations, nor take her into our confidence. "We need a room," I said.

"Sure," she said.

Fumbling with forms and keys took several minutes. I must have glanced anxiously at the doors and windows every few seconds. If Edna noticed, she made no comment. I gave her cash for the room. She gave us a key from a row of mailboxes behind her. Before we left, she winked at us and told us to have a good time.

The key let us through the lobby doors. We walked down faded red carpeting, up a set of creaking wooden stairs, and down faded brown carpeting to a room at the end of the hall.

The room had one regular-sized bed with a salmon-colored chenille bedspread. The carpet was murky green. Two identical pictures of bubbling waterfalls were bolted to opposite walls.

"What is this place?" Scott asked.

I looked at the key. "Says the Luxor," I said.

"Never heard of it."

But I had. Scott hadn't grown up in Chicago and wouldn't

be expected to know, but I did. The Luxor had a reputation in the gay community as a place you could take a prostitute for an hour or two. Look up the word "sleaze" in the dictionary, and you'd find a picture of the Luxor Hotel. Supposedly, there were sex orgies on the roof on hot summer nights. Jockstrap parties on New Year's Eve which could set up a call boy's reputation for years. A Monday-afternoon lavish buffet for the transgender denizens of the hotel and their friends. A leather dungeon where home movies of S/M activity were shown continuously. We had seen absolutely no signs of this tawdry activity as we crossed the lobby. Rotten luck.

I explained about the Luxor's reputation to Scott and finished, "No one would look for us here. We'll be safe for a while."

Scott wandered into the bathroom and returned instantly, shaking his head. I decided not to ask what he'd seen.

"We've got to call the cops," he said.

"Our enemies could be listening on police scanners, figuring since we're good citizens, the logical thing to do would be to call the police. Even if they didn't get here first, all they'd have to do would be to wait until the cops left, and move in. We need to be very careful. Maybe I can call Joe Quinn and explain what happened. They must have gotten calls from people about the traffic problems, and someone must have reported the gunshots. If I call him direct, we won't have to worry about their putting it on the police radio."

"They're probably looking for us for stealing the guy's carriage," Scott said.

"They aren't going to put us in jail for that."

It took nearly fifteen minutes of transferring around for me to get hold of Joe Quinn.

"Where are you?" he demanded.

"If you really wanted to find out," I said, "you could

check the phone records at Eleventh and State and pin-point the origin of this call. Could you just listen for a minute?"

"What the hell happened outside your building?" he asked.

"We're scared," I said. "We aren't at home. I don't think that's safe right now. We don't want anyone to find out where we are."

"Nobody's going to get the phone records to be able to trace the call and even if they could, only I know it's you calling from this number. The person who owns it would be on the screen or printout." As I hesitated he said, "That's as much assurance as I can give."

"Okay," I said and gave him our location.

Quinn added, "Nobody's going to follow me to where you are. We need to talk. Don't go anywhere."

"We're the ones who called you, remember? We want to report this. We didn't do anything wrong."

"I'll be there in fifteen minutes," he said.

It took forty-five minutes for Quinn and Bolewski to show up. Quinn's attitude remained reserved, but I thought willing to listen. Bolewski managed to keep his annoyed-with-us snarl under control. "Hell of a hiding place," Bolewski said.

I stifled my urge to tell him that if he'd feel better we could move to the Ritz. I didn't want to antagonize him.

We had to tell the story three times. They interrupted incessantly with questions.

After we finished explaining, Quinn said, "We were late getting here because we checked the reports about what happened outside your apartment house this morning. The guy from the carriage-rental agency was angry at his driver, the horse, and you."

"I'll buy his goddamn horse and carriage if he wants," Scott said.

"You may have to," Quinn said.

"Also, the media got hold of the story. I don't know if you

were recognized, but nobody is going to be able to keep the name of Scott Carpenter out of the papers if he's connected with a police matter."

"We had to take the horse to escape," I said.

"Not about the horse," Quinn said. "About the guns, shots, and car chase. We had three fender benders, mostly from people gawking at you guys racing down the street. According to witnesses, the guys chasing you didn't get out of traffic until you'd disappeared into Lincoln Park. Said it was quite a sight to see. Whoever the bad guys are, they left some very steamed and frightened motorists at the La Salle and Lake Shore Drive intersection. One guy wanted their insurance information. He got a gun shoved in his face. It'll make all the newscasts. The reporters talked to the eyewitnesses to try and get quotes on camera. They didn't know who you were then, but they will after it's been written up in the police reports."

"So where do we stand?" I asked him. "We're afraid to go back to our place. We can't stay away forever."

"Maybe Carpenter can afford to buy you some protection."

"We can't live with this kind of danger forever," I said. "It must have something to do with Glen Proctor's murder."

We spent an hour going around on that one again.

At the end I said, "Look, the second time, outside our building, obviously they were not afraid of recognition. The question is, why not? They were professionals who didn't have to worry?"

"Wouldn't professionals only take a sure shot in a not-so-public place?" Scott asked.

The cops gave us blank looks. Quinn was nice enough to say, "We don't know."

Bolewski said, "We know something strange is going on. You explained all your logic. I think you know something and you aren't telling."

Scott and I began protests, but Quinn raised his hand.

"Something is not right here," he said. "You guys haven't committed a crime, so we aren't arresting you. The only way we can get information is from you, and you claim you don't know anything. We tried calling other airlines, but none of them has a record of Glen Proctor flying on them anytime in the past two weeks. We'll keep trying to track him down. We'll also go over the statements of everybody who saw anything outside your place, but if their descriptions are anything like yours, we won't have much."

He was referring to our unhelpful eyewitness view of our pursuers. We hadn't had time to examine our attackers, so we hadn't been able to give very good descriptions. I felt foolish, scared, and angry.

"And you'll talk to all the neighbors," I said. "And to the Proctors again?"

"You heard me talk to Mr. Proctor," Quinn said. "As far as he knows, Glen is in Mexico."

"He probably didn't involve his family in whatever he was doing," I said.

"We don't know if there was something he was involved in," Quinn said.

They left after promising to have the local police district give special attention to this street. This meant cop cars would drive down the street more often. Fat lot of good that would do.

The cops left at eleven. We decided to stay at the hotel. It was certainly an unlikely spot for us to be. Not a permanent solution, but it would be as safe as any place for the moment. I found that I was completely exhausted. I checked the sheets on the bed; they were grayish but clean.

Scott yawned and plopped down on the bed. "I really screwed up," he said. "If I hadn't invited Glen Proctor in, none of this would have happened. The murder, the danger to us, trouble with the police, the fight we had. I'm really sorry, Tom."

"We've had fights before," I said. "We've always gotten through them. I was pretty scared a bunch of times in the past few hours. I was glad you were with me. I don't know what I'd ever do without you."

In minutes we slipped under the covers. He lay looking at me with his head propped up on his hand and elbow.

With my fingertips, I caressed his hand that lay on the puce-colored sheet. "What I really want to know is where you learned to drive a horse and buggy that way."

"I'm a farm boy," he said. "I grew up around horses. I did chores until I went to college."

"I knew that," I said. "That still doesn't explain the Roman charioteerlike expertise."

While Scott may have grown up on a farm and been superinvolved in athletics since he was nine. He had attended the University of Arizona on a baseball scholarship. He'd graduated cum laude with a degree in math.

"You never drove a carriage like that on the farm," I said.

"We had trucks," he admitted, "but I figured I'd ridden horses often enough, and we used to play in an old buckboard out in the barn. Wasn't much really to grab the reins and go. I guess I didn't really think much about it."

Scott reached up and flicked off the two lava lamps on the headboard. We moved closer together.

"I'm still scared." Scott's voice murmured against my shoulder.

"Me, too," I said. I held him tight. Usually I can't fall asleep wrapped in his arms, but I was tired, and the warmth and closeness after our adventures felt better than usual. I fell asleep almost instantly.

When I woke up, it was still light. It sounded as if a large chorus was singing ribald songs at the top of their lungs right outside our door. Scott still slept. His ability to sleep through tremendous noise amazes me. I tried rolling over and going back to sleep, but the singing continued. Finally I swung my legs out of bed. I picked up the phone to call the lobby. The noise stopped abruptly. I was too awake to fall back to sleep soon. I called Lester. We needed help, money if we were going to hide out here, maybe a change of clothes. I knew I could trust him.

Lester said, "I have an appointment set up for you with Jason Proctor, head of Proctor International, father of Glen."

"How'd you manage that on a Sunday afternoon?" I asked.

"I have an enormous number of contacts. I made a lot of money for many people, as well as myself. I only had to call in one marker. It was simple."

"What's up?" Scott asked.

I told him about the meeting. Then told Lester what had happened. He hooted loudly when I told him where we were. All he said was, "Both of you are going to need a change of clothes. I can get you clean linen and shirts," Lester said. "They won't be perfect fits, but they'll do." He agreed to drop them off, along with offering us his car. We didn't want to risk returning to our place.

After I hung up, Scott asked, "Do we dare go back to the penthouse?"

"Not-nice people might be watching," I said.

"Why don't they just arrest the people watching our apartment?" Scott asked.

"It's not illegal to sit in a car or be on the street. If we could identify them, it would be different. You can't just yank people off the sidewalk because they look suspicious."

I told him about Lester bringing us clothes and letting us use his car.

"We could rent a car," Scott said.

"We don't know what kind of connections these people have," I said. "If they have access to credit-card computers, they'll be able to pick up our trail."

"They can't have that kind of power."

"I don't want to take any chances."

"We can't walk to Lake Forest," Scott said. "Hell, if it was Monday, I could just go to my bank, withdraw a bundle of cash, and go buy a new car."

"I think the banks are closed tomorrow," I said. "it's Columbus Day weekend. "I don't have school tomorrow either."

Scott sighed. "This is getting far too Byzantine," he said.

"I want to take as few risks as possible."

Lester showed up a half-hour later with clothes and a car. "I love this place," he said. "It brings back fond memories which I have no intention of ever telling anyone about."

In the lobby, Edna gave us a smile and a wave. Outside, the mist and drizzle of earlier had given way to heavy gray clouds and occasional tendrils of fog lurking about the crumbling entrance to the hotel. October was giving its best indication that it was more than ready to ooze into a bleak and dank November.

4

We took Lake Shore Drive to Sheridan Road and on up through the luxury homes that lined the North Shore most of the way to Waukegan. To our east we caught occasional glimpses of the fog-enshrouded lake joining the dark and sodden clouds pouring their gloom toward civilization. Wisps of fog brushed against the Baha'i Temple as we followed the curve of the road into Wilmette. Most of the trees were bare by this time in October, but their number and thickness spoke of tree-lined streets. We passed Tudor, Georgian, and Queen Anne homes of immense size celebrating the wealth of the inhabitants. Luxury mansions and their now-denuded foliage rose in gothic splendor on both sides of the road. The mostly dormant but verdant well-manicured foliage meant that hordes of landscapers could look forward to years of work.

All the times I'd driven up this way, I didn't ever remember seeing a person going into or coming out of one of these homes, much less someone lounging on the lawn or even simply staring out a window. It was as if the inhabitants were as misty and ethereal as the miasma of clouds that were now trying to engulf them.

We got slightly lost as we drove through downtown Highland Park. We passed recently closed Fort Sheridan. Developers slavered over the possibility of grabbing morsels of the property so it could make them richer than they already were.

The funny thing was, I'd grown up in your average middle-class home. On a teacher's salary, I could never possibly have afforded one of these homes. Because of the fortuity of circumstance, I was the lover of one of the highest-paid baseball players in the country. Now we could, if we so chose, live in one of these dream homes.

Just past Lake Forest College, I spotted the turnoff for the Proctor property.

I checked carefully at numerous intervals, but I couldn't detect anyone behind us. Following Lester's directions, we pulled up at a pair of pale brick columns that flanked a vast iron gate. We couldn't see the house because of the six-foot brick wall and dense foliage inside.

I didn't see any button to push to announce our presence. A largish cottage made of the same pale yellow brick as the wall and gate posts stood off to the left inside the walls. An actual lodge keeper emerged from a small door in the overgrown hut and strolled up to the gate. I saw the look in his eyes that I'd seen only in crazed marines in Vietnam just before they marched into the jungle, not caring when or if death dared get in their way. I wouldn't be surprised to see this miscreant in combat fatigues and toting a machine gun. Right now he actually wore an open beige rain slicker over gray pants and a white shirt and black tie.

In a very soft voice, he asked us our business.

We told him we were expected. He told us to wait and took his good time returning to the lodge. He emerged about five minutes later with a large key that he used to unlock a small portion of the gate that was wide enough for only one person to squeeze through at a time. After a searching look behind us along the road, and a few brief words spoken into a walkie-talkie, he slowly pulled out another key, slowly inserted it in the small lock in the center of the gates, and slowly pulled them open.

We drove Lester's silver BMW onto the property. The driveway couldn't have been less than a quarter of a mile long, with nary a pothole or blemish. I assumed it was against the law in these kinds of suburbs to permit such flaws in the pavement.

We arrived at the exterior of a two-story gray brick Gothic Revival home that looked to be sitting on at least an acre of land. To the left I could see tennis courts and an Olympic-sized pool covered for the winter. I saw oak trees of tremendous girth standing as sentinels beside the immense pillar-encrusted square porch. An enormous number of brick chimneys sprouted from the parts of the roof I could see. We pulled up in the circular drive. Before Scott had the engine turned off, a liveried servant emerged from the front door and silently led us up the steps and into the foyer.

This room was three times as big as a school classroom. Double doors led off to rooms left and right. Ahead of us was a grand staircase with halls on either side with openings showing more corridors leading deeper into the house. The servant asked us to wait and left us.

The floor was lined with broken granite and marble mosaics laid in a star pattern. At regular intervals, bronze vases filled with artificial flowers lined the walls. A ten-foot-by-ten-foot Rubenesque painting featured a woman with naked breasts and well-rounded rear, surrounded by flowing robes. It dominated the room from its location on the right-hand wall.

Scott nodded toward the painting. "I bet it's not a reproduction," he said.

The set of doors on the left slid open silently. A man in his early twenties looked at us, glanced up the stairs and down both hallways, and then beckoned us over.

Everything he wore was white: shorts, shirt, socks, shoes, with a towel draped around his neck. He had the lightest-gold blond hair I had ever seen. It was cut short on the sides, and the wispy waves on top were something I could have buried my nose in and run my fingers through a thousand times. His stomach was flat; his calf muscles and biceps stood out with definition but not bulk. As we neared him, he turned sideways for more-anxious looks up the stairs and hall. His butt had the same perfect round-ness of Glen Proctor's. The blond hair and the swath of freckles across his nose that his perfect tan couldn't hide told me this had to be a close relation.

He confirmed this by saying, "I'm Glen's brother, Bill. I don't want anyone seeing me with you, but I've got to talk to you when you're done with my father."

"About what?" I asked.

"No time now. I'll find you after you're done." He shut the doors.

"He's beautiful," I said.

"He looks a lot like Glen," Scott said. "You didn't think he was so hot-looking."

"I never said Glen wasn't hot, but this guy is perfection."

Scott raised an amused eyebrow. "Are you smitten?"

"I recognize perfection. Half the faggots in the city would pay a fortune to go to bed with that guy. Artists would flock to sculpt his figure."

"Maybe they already do," Scott said.

I shook myself. "He's scared about something."

"How are we going to talk to him in secret if servants greet us at the door, and a gatekeeper is blocking the entrance? They must have people spying out of every nook and cranny."

"I don't know," I said. "I said he was beautiful. I don't know how bright he is, but he may know or suspect some-thing. We've got to try to talk to him."

We heard a discreet cough and turned to see the servant who led us in standing near the bottom of the stairs. He beckoned with his white-gloved hand. We followed him down the hallway to the right of the grand staircase, made a right turn halfway down, then through a door to another hall that led past numerous closed doors. This corridor had dark maroon carpeting and was hung with impressionist paintings, each with its own brass-covered light.

The servant, a man in his mid-thirties, opened a door at the end of this passage and said, "This way gentlemen."

We strode though the entry into a room that let in tons of light through floor-to-ceiling picture windows in both walls. A tall man with gold hair flecked with silver held out his hand to us. He introduced himself as Jason Proctor and murmured polite greetings. When I glanced around the room, I realized that the servant was gone. I hadn't heard him leave.

The focal point of the room was a thirty-foot stone fireplace. The sofa across from it was only long enough for one baseball team to take naps on at a time. Another wall had a pine media cabinet with a branch bench nestled nearby. Easy chairs in the same plush fabric as the sofa were spaced around the room and against the walls. Hand-woven silk pillows clustered at various points on the couch and loungers. Brass fish on stands gathered on one end table and three enameled spheres rested on another. The coffee table had an enormous collection of dried flowers in a gargantuan brass pot. Wicker chairs and an oak coffee table along with wooden beams in the ceiling added to the rustic effect. One could get lost in and read books forever in the comfortableness of these surroundings. Scott was rich, but this was real money spent to feel comfortable and luxurious at the same time.

Jason Proctor wore a white button-down shirt, peeking from under a gray cashmere sweatshirt sweater that zipped up the front, beige slacks, gray and red socks, and Loro Piana gray cashmere slippers.

Proctor led us to the couch. He took a seat opposite on a lounge chair.

"Mr. Carpenter," Proctor said, "I have followed your baseball career for many years. I am an admirer, although

I admit I don't attend many games. I've often thought of buying a team. I did watch the seventh game of the World Series you pitched several years ago. Magnificent."

They talked baseball for a few minutes.

"And you, sir?" Proctor turned to me.

"He's my lover," Scott said.

"I'm a schoolteacher in the south suburbs," I said. And somehow felt foolish for saying so. I guess the surroundings intimidated me more than I thought.

Proctor gave no indication that our being lovers made a difference to him.

"Teaching is a noble and highly underpaid profession," Proctor said. He managed to sound paternal, but not condescending. I wondered whether it was a trick he had.

Scott said, "We're here about your son."

"Yes. I'm aware of what you say happened. The police called, and your friend Lester mentioned it. We have been in almost continuous contact with the police in Chicago and in Mexico. I talked with the team owners this morning."

Apparently Jason Proctor didn't have to go through intermediaries.

"We can confirm that he is not with the team at the moment," Proctor said.

"We aren't lying about what we saw," I said.

He studied us for several moments. The flesh on his face was still taut, and his frame was well muscled, if beginning to sag a little in the middle. He was in good shape, and I could see where his sons got their athleticism. When he was younger, he might have been as attractive as the son who'd met us in the hall earlier. He trained his sharp blue eyes on us.

"I cannot believe something has happened to my son," Proctor said.

I felt as if I were trying to fill Lake Michigan with a thimble, but how can you press a parent when you are bringing the news of the death of a child?

"I know this can be difficult, sir," I said, "but do you have any idea if Glen was in some kind of trouble, doing anything illegal?"

"I have no idea. He has had troubles before, as everyone knows, but I thought after this last time he was clean. I had hoped so. I talked to him two weeks ago before he left for Mexico, and all we talked about was the team, baseball, and his prospects for the coming season."

"Do you know if he had any other plans while he was in Mexico?" I asked. "Something to do with your businesses?"

"He might have spent some time with some of my executives," Proctor said. "A few of them have been down there looking for ideal locations to build. We'll be moving more operations down there now, with the North American Free Trade Agreement. I often had Glen work for me. I wanted to help him. Give him a sense of responsibility."

"Did he have any enemies here or in Mexico?" Scott asked.

"None that I know of," Proctor said. "This is difficult for me to discuss with you gentlemen. I understand you were friends with my son, and if your news is true, it will be a . . . crushing . . . unbelievable blow. Please understand, I don't mean to denigrate what you've said or your intentions, but I have a large number of business dealings in Mexico, and I'm having everything there examined carefully. If Glen is dead, and if he was in trouble in Mexico, I want to find out about it first—not read it in some sleazy tabloid."

"Your son *is* dead, Mr. Proctor," I said.

His eyes lit on mine and kept their gaze there. He looked away first. I saw his hand tremble. "We'll have to see what the future brings," was all he said.

He pressed a button on the side of his chair and stood up. I had a lot of other questions, but the interview was obviously over.

I didn't know the servant had entered until Proctor said, "James, please see these men out."

He shook our hands, wished us luck, and we were out the door.

Halfway down the hall, I said to the servant, "James, when was the last time you saw Glen?"

His voice was correctly cold and disapproving when he said, "I'm sure Mr. Proctor has answered all of your questions."

I didn't bother to ask again. James let us out the front door. As I put the key in the car door, a voice called to us. I looked up and saw Bill Proctor beckoning to us from the side of the house. We joined him there.

Proctor said, "I knew James wouldn't let you out of his sight. He's a nosy old queen."

"So are we," I said.

Proctor raised an eyebrow, but he said, "I wanted to catch you here. Dad has a whole mess of guards. 'Way before Ross Perot brought his paranoia thing to national attention, Dad was heavily invested in protection. Of course, my dad's not as rich as Ross."

Bill Proctor led us to a side door, down a hall, and up a staircase. This hall matched the others for simple elegance. Proctor addressed comments to Scott as he led us. "My brother told me you were his best friend on the team. That you were the only one who stood by him when he got suspended the first time. He also said you were a fag." At my frown Proctor said. "Sorry. That's what he called you. That's kind of what you said a few minutes ago. Are you guys really gay? I didn't believe him when he told me Scott Carpenter was gay. Hard to believe a professional baseball player bends over. Kinda unbelievable."

Scott stopped in the middle of the hall. You couldn't hear a sound in the entire house. Scott and I looked at each other, then back at Proctor.

Scott said, "Sometimes I bend over, sometimes Tom

does. If we're really in the mood, we both do at the same time. It's magic."

"Oh!" Proctor said.

I let silence build for a minute, then said, "You wanted our help?"

"Yeah, right." He cleared his throat, then continued down the hall to the last door on the right.

"This is the room Glen grew up in as a kid," Proctor said as he opened the door.

Glen's room had a king-sized bed with a quilted flannel bedspread, made of warm autumn colors. He had a dresser and a chest of drawers of solid oak. The carpet was deep plush gold. The white walls over the bed were filled with pictures of all the big-name athletes of the past fifty years. One other wall was filled with a fantastic array of posters of unicorns. On top of the dresser were a wide variety of bongs and water pipes. An open door off to the left showed a bathroom with a sunken tub. In a sitting area opposite this door were a brown leather couch and two matching chairs. A large picture window had let Glen look out on the world. Outside I could see the wisps of fog had changed into a thickening mist. Visibility was maybe a hundred feet. I could make out thirty or forty feet of relatively calm lake. The waves barely brushed the shore. Hardly a ripple disturbed the cold gray surface. I could see the dim outline of a pier with one boat anchored at each side and one at the far end.

"I didn't mean to insult you guys back there," Proctor said.

"What did you want?" I asked.

"I need to talk. Something screwy is going on. My father told me that you were coming and that it was about Glen, but he wouldn't say what. I'm worried about him."

Obviously his dad hadn't told him about what we'd reported to the police. His manner certainly didn't seem to include sorrow or suffering. He was more like a kid who had been playing a prank and was worried about how much trouble he might be in.

He'd changed into blue jeans and running shoes. He wore a white fisherman's sweater partially covered with a blue denim jacket.

He leaned back in the chair. "I don't trust my dad or the servants. I've got no one else to turn to. I need your help."

First the one brother and then the other. Who knew how alike they might be? No matter how pretty he was, I wasn't prepared to trust him very far or help very much until it was proven to me that we could trust him.

I said, "You better not be trying to jerk us around."

Scott said, "That's awful harsh, Tom."

"I don't know who I trust at the moment," I said to him. Then I turned to Proctor. "I'm not sure what your game is, but we've been chased and shot at, and I'm not willing to take any chances at the moment."

"Is this necessary, Tom?" Scott asked.

"Yes," I said. I was fully prepared to list the problems his sympathy had gotten us into. At this point, all precautions were to be taken.

"Look," Proctor said, "I really think Glen's in trouble, and I don't know what to do."

He looked and sounded sincere. His brother was dead, and he had sounded as if he genuinely cared about him.

"I don't know what to do to get you to trust me," he said. "My dad said you had news about my brother. What's happened?"

"I'm sorry," I said. "We've got bad news." Suddenly I felt ashamed and awkward. Here I had been bullying some probably-innocent kid, to whom we were about to give perfectly awful news.

"I'm sorry," I repeated as if my sorrow could take some of the sting away. "We found your brother last night at Scott's. He'd been shot through . . ." I paused, cleared my throat, shook my head. "He was dead."

"No," Proctor said.

"I'm sorry," I said and felt silly for saying it for the third time, but I don't know anyone who has the perfect words for horrific moments like this.

Tears came to his eyes. "I really loved him. I've looked up to him ever since I can remember." He turned away from us. Tears flowed down his face. "I can't believe it."

His shoulders began to shake. Scott reached out, and the kid sagged into his arms.

I felt awful for him. I know I'd be devastated if I found out one of my brothers or my sister was dead.

Scott held Proctor, patting the blond hair, rubbing his hand in a circle on the back of his jacket.

I wondered whether his dick was getting hard and felt like a crude creep for thinking such a thought.

Proctor's crying turned to sniffles and muted gulps for air. "This is awful," he said. "What happened?"

I told him about his brother and gave him a brief synopsis of our adventures.

As I spoke about Glen, tears made occasional forays down Bill's cheeks. He didn't seem to have a hankie, but wiped his jacket sleeve across his nose and snuffled deeply.

After I finished, Proctor stared out at the silent vapors gathering outside. Periodically he snorted the snot in his nose and tamped at the occasional tear that still escaped.

"I'm sorry about your brother," I said.

I got a brief nod in response. We sat in silence for some minutes until Proctor asked, "You know what I remember most about him?"

I shook my head.

"He was only a year older than me, so we did a lot of things together, but the best was Christmas. We'd hunt through the house room by room searching for the presents. We'd always find some, but then, Christmas morning, he'd come into my room and wake me up, and we'd be the first ones to the Christmas tree, like all kids, but it was always just the two of us with the enormous Christmas tree, lights still off, faint gray light coming through the windows, us still in our pajamas, and we'd search for the presents with each others' names on them, and we'd make piles around us, and forts, and shoot silent guns, because we didn't want anyone to hear us, and then we'd combine our packages into one big fort and nestle inside and tell secrets and guess what was inside the packages, what we'd asked for and hoped for, and when your dad is as rich as ours, more often than not, our wildest dreams came true."

He dried a few more tears with his jacket. "He was the best brother," Proctor said. "I hated it every year when he went away to school.

"You attended school here?" I asked.

"I went to the public schools on the North Shore. There aren't many better private schools, and I wanted to be with kids I knew. My parents didn't have a lot of choice with Glen. A lot of schools kicked him out. Even Dad with all his money couldn't keep him in. Glen had some brave teachers in kindergarten and first grade. They forced my parents to come in for conferences. Glen was impossible. He was always good to me, but we lost several servants because they wouldn't put up with the way he treated them even when he was five or six, but Dad's money always prevailed. It always has."

My dislike for Glen Proctor and his privilege burst out in almost-unwonted sarcasm. "Poor little rich boy," I said.

"Tom!" Scott said.

"It's all right," Proctor said. "I was lucky to have a rich dad. I don't hate him for that. Glen loved him. When we were kids, they always hung around together. Glen was oldest, and I guess that was special to my father."

He stopped talking and I let the silence continue. Finally he asked me, "What did my dad say when you told him?"

"I don't think he believed us."

"Typical. He thinks his money will buy anything. There

aren't enough men and horses in his kingdom to put back his son's life."

"Why wouldn't he believe us?" I asked.

"I stopped trying to understand my dad years ago. I live in a separate world. I'll see him occasionally at breakfast like today, but that's about it."

"What kind of trouble do you think Glen might have been in? We've been trying to figure out who might have killed him and who would be after us. You know anything about what he's been up to lately?"

"I don't know about recent danger. When we were kids, he was always the one of us who tried the most daring or new or unusual thing. He'd jump first, climb first, dive off first. He got me my first beer, my first hit of dope, showed me how to beat off, got me my first condom."

"What kind of trouble did he get into in school?" I asked.

"I remember he got suspended one time in first grade for telling the teacher, the principal, and the social worker to fuck off."

"Not a usual first-grader's response to stimuli," I said.

"No," Proctor admitted. "Let me think what other stuff he used to do." He strode to the window and wiped the sleeve of his jacket on the window as if to clear away the mist gathering outside. He spoke without turning around. "One time he threw a condom at the second-grade teacher. It was her first job out of college, and she couldn't cope with him. I heard she ran down the hall shrieking, although that could just have been Glen exaggerating. I know she didn't teach the next year in that school.

"I remember he used to steal a lot of stuff. One time I asked him why, since we had so much at home. He said he liked to. It was fun to see all the grown-ups and the kids go nuts trying to find things, or make things right, or fix things."

"This happen when he went away to school?" I asked.

Bill turned back to us and sat back down. "I'm not sure. I think he found other things to get in trouble about."

"Drugs?" I said.

Proctor nodded. "And alcohol. I used to watch him sneak drinks before, during, and after family holiday parties. He must have been five or six the first time I saw him do it. Once in a while he'd offer me some, but I hated the taste. He started on drugs in fifth or sixth grade when he was away at school. He came back one summer and introduced me to pot. I smoked a few times with him and his buddies each summer, but I didn't see him as much as he got older, because he was into baseball so much. I had lots of other sports, crafts, classes, and special trips. Thinking back on it, my parents probably planned it so I'd have less contact with him. I seemed to be in a lot more activities than most of my friends every summer."

"He ever do harder drugs?" I asked.

"Cocaine and marijuana, mostly," Proctor said. "He never did anything else in front of me. Claimed he wasn't an addict, before and after he went away for rehab. The family kept it real quiet, and with Dad's money, that means total silence. Nobody knew Glen went away after sophomore and junior years in high school to some clinic. I think the baseball people would have hesitated if they'd known about his problem."

"Would have avoided him completely," Scott said.

"What I remember most was the fun times. The wild things he did." Proctor nearly smiled.

"Like what?" I asked.

Bill was silent for a minute. Then smiled. "One time we were at some friends' house in Wisconsin. Glen didn't have his driver's license yet, so he must have been about fifteen. The kids we were staying with weren't old enough to drive, either, but we took the car one afternoon. We drove to some railroad tracks, and the other kids suggested we let half the air out of the tires and drive along the tracks. Glen did. I remember the wild sensation of flying down the tracks barely feeling the bump of the ties. It was a convertible, and Glen had real long hair at the time. His hair flew in the wind as he laughed and sang."

"No train came?" Scott said.

"No, Glen's luck always seemed to run that way, even with some of the dumbest stuff he did. He finally graduated high school from an exclusive place somewhere in Vermont. I think my dad had to promise them a huge endowment for them to let him be in the ceremony and graduate on time. For a celebration we had half the kids on the North Shore at this big bonfire on the beach. It was great. Glen was drunk and nobody else was feeling a lot of pain, when Glen took a lighter out and casually set his chest hair on fire."

"He did what?" I asked.

"Swear to God," Bill said. "Just casually flicked it on and applied it to his chest."

"How come his chest hair didn't just go foof with him going up in flames? That can't be just luck."

"One guy threw a glass of beer on Glen, but it missed the flames. Actually what happens is the hair kind of curls in on itself and melts and the fire goes out. It's hair spray and stuff that makes it go foof in flames."

I was flabbergasted, but I believed Glen Proctor would do something that crazy. I didn't stop Bill from talking. I might be impatient about getting us out of danger, but I hoped Bill might actually mention something that could help us. And the man had his grief to work out. If he could remember with smiles and tears, then that was okay.

"Didn't he ever get caught?" Scott asked.

"Never for the really big stuff," Bill said. "He came close once when he almost got busted for a huge drug shipment."

I raised an eyebrow. "What happened?"

"He must have been sixteen. He'd gone down to Mexico for a month. My dad has lots of business down there, so we went pretty often. How Glen got to know the local drug people, I don't know. He always seemed to be able to know people with illegal secrets and deals. Glen agreed to have a huge shipment of drugs sent back across the border with some stuff for my father. Glen almost got caught."

"By the cops?" I asked.

"No. My dad's security forces. He has a lot down there. Glen managed to get the shipping invoice changed, like maybe seconds before he would have been discovered. I think the head of security was awful suspicious. Maybe Glen paid him off some way. I don't know. Anyhow, the stuff got to Chicago, the drug guys got their shipment, and Glen got enough stuff to supply his whole school for a semester." Bill was silent for a minute. He sighed and tears started again. "Mostly his schemes seemed to work."

"Whatever this one was," Scott said, "it went bust big-time."

"Yeah," Proctor said. The tears came again. "He really loved me," Bill said. "One summer when I was twelve, he and I hot-wired some farm equipment and drove it around in the middle of the night. It was my idea and I got them started. Glen took the blame for me. I was too scared to speak up. And when I was sixteen, the first girl I loved broke up with me. Glen stayed with me the whole night. I loved her so bad, and Glen was so good. He helped me a lot. I really loved him." He shut his eyes and sobbed. Scott held him briefly.

It was nearly nine o'clock. I wasn't eager to go back to our hotel room, but I didn't see any alternative. We stayed a few more minutes to comfort Bill Proctor and told him if we found anything out we'd let him know. He promised to do the same. By ten we'd driven through the drive-up window at a fast-food restaurant and arrived back at our hotel.

Edna was still on duty at the desk when we returned. The lobby had a collection of transvestites and prostitutes, the tame version of which you've seen on Phil Donahue and Geraldo.

In our room we sat on the bed and ate greasy hamburgers. When we finished, I tried calling our answering machine. I got the distinct bong from AT&T, then punched in my code number.

I listened to the beginning of the message on our machine and then punched the two-number code that gave access to the messages. Scott lay down next to me on the bed. I listened to his breathing in the pauses between messages. The hotel itself was amazingly quiet for the moment.

One message was from Lester, asking us how we'd done and to give him a call. Another was a woman's voice, who said her name was Felicia Proctor, Glen's and Bill's mother. A third was from Brad—no last name—telling Glen he was at the Hotel Chicago and he had to talk to him.

Next I tried calling the cops in Chicago. I got Joe Quinn at his desk. I told him about our conversations at the Proctors. He seemed slightly interested in that.

He said, "We've tried to find out what we could about who attacked you on the street this morning, but I gotta tell you, we've got nothing. I don't think we're going to get much."

"We obviously need protection. A crime is trying to happen. Us getting killed."

Quinn said, "I don't mean to be rude, but your buddy Carpenter could afford to hire an army. We're poor cops with a lot of real crimes and cases to solve."

"We're scared," I said. "We're stuck in this dump, and we don't dare return home. What do you suggest we do?"

"I don't know," he said.

I called our lawyer. I like my legal talent to be nice and conservative and that's what my lawyer was. Todd Bristol had been my lawyer since before I met Scott. Now we kept him on a yearly retainer. He was a partner in one of the big law firms on La Salle Street.

I caught him on the way out to a party. As soon as he knew it was me, he covered the phone, but I heard his muffled voice say, "This is going to take a while. You'd better grab a cab and go ahead. I'll be there as soon as I can."

I knew Todd hated parties in direct proportion to his lover Ed's passion for them. Todd wouldn't mind missing any portion of it.

"What is going on?" he asked. "The radio is filled with crazy stories. Reporters are dying to talk to you guys."

"What have they said?" I asked.

"One of your neighbors swore he saw Scott driving one of those carriages down the Inner Drive like somebody out of one of those Roman chariot races."

I explained everything to him from the beginning. He listened without interruption.

When I finished, he said, "Where are the necklaces?"

"Mine's in the penthouse. Scott must still be wearing his."

"Get them to a safety-deposit box, or someplace reasonably safe as soon as you can."

"I'm worried about going to the penthouse," I said.

"You could try going in with a police escort," Todd suggested, "or wait, then whoever is after you will just pick up your trail again. I think those necklaces are a menace."

"You think they're the key?"

"I don't know, but that's the most obvious place to start, although it would have made a lot more sense if whoever was after you simply said, 'Could we have our necklaces back, please?' Of course, yours may be gone already."

I told him I wanted to call Lester to get more information about the Proctor family and their wealth.

"Does he know where you are?"

"Yes."

"I wish nobody knew. Don't tell anybody else—including me—where you are. Not even your best friend. Something loony is going on. You cannot be too careful."

"I've known Lester for years," I said.

"Have you been chased and shot at? Have these people shown a tendency to be nasty and persistent? Come on, Tom. Use your head. You're frightened, aren't you?"

"Yes."

"Good. Then use that fear to be supremely cautious. The cops are probably all right, but don't take any chances."

"What should we do?" I asked.

"Figure out who's behind all this. Find out what they want, and if at all possible, give it to them; and if it is impossible, try to make a deal."

"We need to find out about Glen Proctor's movements in Mexico and what he was really there for," I said.

"I don't think I can help you there, but I'll make a few discreet calls in case there are skeletons in that closet. With all that money and all the enemies he's made, Jason Proctor's got to be hated by a whole lot of people."

I thanked him and hung up, then called Lester.

"What happened at Proctor's?" he asked.

Something about his eagerness made me wary, or was it that Todd had sufficiently frightened me into general paranoia? I gave him a brief outline of our two discussions. I asked, "Can you find out about any real-estate dealings old man Proctor had in Mexico? The reason his kid died and why we're being stalked has got to be connected with what Glen was doing in Mexico."

"You could go down there and try to track his movements," Lester said.

I'd thought of it, and I supposed we could, but I'd rather not be snooping around in a foreign country, where I didn't know the language or any of the people. At least here I knew people and could call for help. I explained all that to Lester.

"You're right," he said. He promised to do what he could to find out about Proctor senior's dealings in Mexico.

I sat near the head of the bed and leaned my back against the wall. I was totally bushed. I gazed out the window to the brick wall next to us.

"I'm tired," Scott said.

"You and Glen know somebody named Brad?"

"Brad who?"

I explained about the message on the machine.

"Only Brad I know is a guy from Glen's rookie year. He used to pal around with Brad Stawalski who was kind of big and goofy and not real bright. The kind of guy you play practical jokes on. Stuck with the team that year for a few months because our regular first baseman was injured. They were roommates."

"Did they keep in touch?"

"Glen didn't mention him before he was killed."

I tried calling the Hotel Chicago for Brad Stawalski. He was registered, but his room didn't answer.

"Do we go chasing after him tonight?" Scott asked. "We've only had a few hours' sleep, and I'm too wiped out. We don't know when he'll be back or even if he knew anything about what happened to Glen."

We agreed to check on him tomorrow.

With the lights out, we got only a faint glow from outside through the torn gauze of the curtains. Our view was of a brick wall two feet away. We stripped to our underwear and crawled into bed. The pillows were nearly flat. The metal joists of the bed stabbed my back through the thin mattress. My feet hung over the end. I thought it was heavenly to relax.

Scott snuggled close, lying on his side next to me while I lay on my back. I could feel his legs and chest warm against my own, along with his arm draped over my chest, and his chin on my shoulder.

I reached over with my right hand and ran my fingertips down his arm to the elbow, then over to his side, down his torso to his waist, and then to his hips, where the cotton waistband of his tight white Jockey shorts met his skin. I let my fingers rove down the waistband to where it stretched and made a bridge over his flat abdomen then over to where skin met material again. I heard his breathing quicken in my ear, felt his desire with my hand.

I turned toward Scott and pulled him close. I listened to the sounds of air being taken into and being expelled from his lungs. I put my hand on his chest, felt the golden downy fur and the slightly freckled skin, and beneath it the beating heart. I sighed deeply. I was incredibly tired. I felt myself dropping off to my favorite fantasy of making love to Scott on the pitching mound, after he hurled a complete game victory, and he would pull me to him, and he'd be all sweaty and happy about winning, and he'd kiss me passionately in front of his assembled teammates and thronged fans.

5

I woke the next morning to Scott sitting on the side of the bed, his hand resting on my shoulder. I felt comfortably warm. He had dressed in the same clothes he had worn yesterday. He needed a shave and a shower although his five o'clock shadow was incredibly sexy. I got up, dressed, and made a foray to the bathroom. It was the kind of space that it was better not to turn the light on in, much less inspect closely. It had only a toilet and a washstand. Where the tub might have been was a gaping space with a small circular hole in the ground where a pipe might once have been.

I called the Hotel Chicago number the mystery man had left. Brad Stawalski was still registered at the hotel, but his room did not answer. No one at the desk knew where he was or when he might be in; but check-out time was noon, so he'd have to have contacted someone by that point. I left Glen's name as the person who was calling.

I tried the number for Mrs. Proctor. The answering-service person, who had a nasal voice and should have been chewing gum, said that Mrs. Proctor was not in but she had left a message that we could come by after two that afternoon and meet with her. I didn't like the idea of meeting anyone in a set place where a trap could be sprung on us. I wrote down the address.

The lobby of the hotel was deserted. No one sat behind

the registration desk. I paused at the door and searched the street. As I was about to open the door, I thought I caught a glimpse of a dark sedan with two men sitting in front parked illegally half a block down.

"Trouble?" Scott asked.

"I don't know, but let's not risk it. There's got to be a back way out of this place." The alley behind the hotel was as unsavory as the inside, but it was empty of possible killers. Maybe the two I'd seen out front hadn't been bad guys or had anything to do with us. If they were, wouldn't they have had someone in the alley? I hoped I was right, but didn't mind taking the precaution.

On our way to the hotel, Scott asked, "What if someone gets into the penthouse and listens to the messages? Won't they be able to track down this Brad Stawalski, too."

"I used the touch tones on the phone to erase the messages last night."

"Somebody could have already gotten them," Scott said.

"They wouldn't be expecting us to get calls. I don't want our only option to be total paralysis based on fear. We just have to be extremely cautious."

We grabbed a cup of coffee from the Rock-and-Roll Mc-Donald's on Ontario Street.

We parked on Kinzie Street west of Wells right behind the Merchandise Mart. We walked east to Dearborn and up to the Hotel Chicago.

The Hotel Chicago was the newest, most exclusive, and most modern hotel in Chicago. It was just north of the Hotel Nikko and across from Marina City.

"How are we going to meet him without alerting our pursuers?" Scott asked.

"Simple," I said. I checked my watch. "We'll set up a rendezvous point. Then, instead of being there to meet him, we'll shadow him and see if anybody is stalking him. If they are, we'll call it off."

"Won't they be just as likely to kill him as they did Glen?" Scott asked.

"I hope he's not dead yet, although I'm sure he's in danger, but we've got to try."

In the lobby we found the pay phones. First I called the penthouse. Glen had another message from Brad. He said he'd be in his room from ten to twelve and then would be checking out. He sounded extremely frightened.

I relayed the information to Scott.

"He still doesn't know Glen's dead?" Scott asked.

"Hard to tell," I said. "I think you better call him. He'll recognize your voice. I'm hoping he'll trust you enough to meet us."

"Do I tell him about Glen?"

"Not yet," I said.

This time someone in the room picked up the phone. I listened to Scott introduce himself. I caught the syncopated effect of listening to one-half of a phone conversation.

"This is Scott Carpenter . . . I'm calling for Glen Proctor. . . . He's in trouble . . . He wants you to meet him on the steps of the Art Institute at eleven . . . Michigan and Adams . . . Big building, takes up most of the block on the east side of the street . . . I can't tell you over the phone. . . . We'll talk when we meet. . . ." He hung up.

"Our Brad isn't an art lover," I said.

"Never heard of the place," Scott said. "He may not be too bright, but he knows enough that he should be scared. Now what?"

"He still hasn't been captured or spotted, or he'd have suffered Glen's fate."

"What if they're using him as bait to get to us?" Scott asked.

"We're reversing the process. If someone is after him, we follow him *and* them. We can follow them back to their source, but he's got to still be free of them. They wouldn't let him live."

"What if they try to kill Brad?" Scott asked. "Do we let them and then follow them to get ourselves killed? We should tell the cops about this Brad guy and let them question him. We can make a call to Quinn. He can follow up."

As we talked, I maneuvered so we could see the elevators.

"What crime is it that we'd be reporting?" I asked. "That this guy left a message for Glen on our machine? That is not a violation of criminal statutes as far as I can tell."

"Won't they want to talk to anyone who can give them information about Glen's death?" Scott asked.

"Brad probably thinks he's alive. According to the cops, he's not dead, remember? Maybe they think we're the ones who have fallen afoul of some criminal organization for reasons that we are unable or unwilling to tell them."

"What if he just skips town and doesn't go to the Art Institute?" Scott asked.

"If this doesn't work, we'll try something else. Maybe you could come up with an idea that keeps us safe, has the cops take us seriously, and solves Glen's murder. I'd be happy to hear any suggestions." I surprised myself with my vehemence and sarcasm.

"I'm sorry," Scott began. Then an extremely muscular man with slicked-back black hair, wearing running shoes, blue jeans, and a sweatshirt, walked off the elevator. He headed straight for the door and turned south.

"That's him," Scott said and began to follow.

"Wait," I said.

I let my eyes rove over the characters seated in the lobby. Two men in business suits chatted near the potted palm. One in a Ralph Lauren warm-up suit strode toward the elevators. A couple in their late teens or early twenties talked earnestly with a blue-rinsed matron, perhaps their grandmother or a maiden aunt. A bellhop moved a flatcar of luggage toward the street. No one seemed to take any notice of us or Brad Stawalski. Certainly no one wearing sunglasses and toting a machine gun burst out from behind a pillar and started spraying the lobby with unpleasantness.

I waited another minute; then we spun through the revolving doors. The doorman at the curb asked if we needed a cab. I spotted Brad on foot at the midpoint on the bridge crossing over the Chicago River. I told the doorman no on the cab.

We moved a few steps away from the door. I turned to Scott and said, "Let's pretend we're having a pleasant casual conversation. Each of us carefully looks over the parked cars and pedestrians in our view."

"What are we looking for?"

"Anything that looks remotely suspicious."

Several minutes' observation revealed nothing.

"We'll lose him if we wait much longer," Scott said.

I looked toward the river. Stawalski had reached the red light at Wacker Drive. I could tell he wasn't a native Chicagoan because he waited for the light to change before he began to cross. Good Chicago street crossers, if they see the slightest chance to take a step or two ahead, are already well off the curb and daring traffic.

Glancing at my watch, I saw we had nearly half an hour before the appointed time. Brad seemed in no particular hurry although he checked every corner and looked back several times to see whether he was being followed. We crossed to the east side of the street, strolled easily, and kept to shadows and gazed in windows, doing everything but holding hands to show that we couldn't possibly be following him.

As we crossed Randolph Street, he disappeared to our west on the farther side of the Daley Center. He had turned the wrong direction for the Art Institute. We poked along until we could see through the glass in the Daley Center to the plaza with the enormous Picasso statue of whatever-it-was-supposed-to-be. I spotted Stawalski among the tourists gaping up at the construction.

We continued on past the plaza while Brad lingered to gawk. The autumn sky was gray, but the day had warmed up and the wind was calm. We walked with our jackets open.

I guided us west on Washington Street until we were halfway through the next block, with City Hall bulking large on our right. We crossed the street and ambled back. All the while I kept my eye out for anyone too interested in Brad. So far nothing. We hung around the Miró sculpture and watched Brad stare at pigeons for a few minutes until he moved south on Dearborn once more. We watched everybody who fell in behind him for the next few minutes, even the people on cross streets, and as well as we could those in cabs and cars. We saw nothing suspicious.

We moved back to Dearborn. We strode past the First National Bank building, the Chagall Wall, crossed Monroe Street, past the Xerox Centre, to Adams Street, where Brad turned east toward the Art Institute. We crossed to the south side of Adams and followed. The mid-morning Monday crowds were thick enough so that we easily blended in. Brad now rarely checked to see if he was being followed.

We crossed State Street and then Wabash Avenue. As we neared Michigan, Brad slowed perceptibly, then ducked into the Burger King on the corner of Adams and Michigan.

I pulled Scott into the alley between Wabash and Michigan Avenue. "Let's meet him in the Burger King," I said. "We haven't seen anybody the least bit suspicious, except maybe ourselves and him. He'll recognize you, so he won't be inclined to run. This is good enough."

Inside Brad sat at a corner table with a soft drink in front of him. Most of the time he watched the steps of the Art Institute across Michigan Avenue. He didn't notice us until our shadows fell across his line of vision.

He leaped to his feet. He stared at me, then caught sight of Scott and gave him a weak smile.

Scott introduced us. We all shook hands and sat down.

"What is going on?" Brad asked. "I've been trying to get hold of Glen. When I call his dad's place, they won't give me any information. I called the number he gave me to get hold of him. That must have been you guys?"

Scott nodded.

"What is going on?" Brad repeated.

"Glen is dead," Scott said.

"He can't be," Brad said. "It's not possible. He finally had everything together. He'd made his last deal. He was going to stop living on the edge."

Scott told him what we'd found.

Brad shook his head. "It can't be. Why didn't they tell me when I called the house?"

Scott explained what we knew about the situation in the Proctor home.

"This is crazy," Brad said. "You say you saw him?"

"I saw the bullet holes," I said. "I touched the body."

Scott nodded confirmation.

Brad pointed at me. "Who are you? Scott introduced you, but you're not a baseball player, although you've got the build for it."

"Scott and I are lovers."

Brad stared at Scott. "I heard the rumors you were gay. I want you to know I never believed them. I never spread them."

"What's important now," Scott said, "is figuring out who killed Glen, who is after us, and from the way you've been acting, who is after you."

"Yeah," he said. "Something screwy is going on. Just after I crossed the border back into the United States, a bunch of guys with guns seized the bus from Mexico. I could have been on it but I'd decided to drive over and see a former girlfriend of mine in Houston then fly up from there. From what you told me about Glen, I'm glad I wasn't on that bus."

"Were you and Glen traveling together in Mexico?" I asked.

"Yeah," Brad said.

"But you didn't come back together?" Scott asked.

"Glen thought we shouldn't," Brad said.

"You said he made his last deal and that he was going to stop living on the edge. What deal?" I asked.

Brad gave a shrug of his massive shoulders, scratched his slicked-back hair, and glanced fearfully out the window.

"I don't know if I can tell," Brad said.

"Why not?" Scott asked.

"It's real complicated." Brad eyed each passerby suspiciously, pulled out a handkerchief, and wiped sweat from his forehead and above his lip.

"You're really scared," I said.

"Glen was supposed to call the cops," Brad said. "He was going to arrange protection."

"What was going on in Mexico?" Scott said.

"I'm scared," Brad said. "I hate being in this public place."

We debated briefly about where to go. Brad suggested his hotel room. I vetoed that as too dangerous. I didn't want Brad to know where our temporary refuge was. Scott suggested my lawyer's office. I called, but got his answering service at work and his machine at home.

Finally I said, "I know the perfect place." I saw an empty cab at the corner waiting for the light. "Follow me!" I ordered. I dashed out of the restaurant and flung open the cab door. As we piled in, I did a quick reconnaissance of the nearby populace. An art student hurried by with her four-by-five-foot flat leather case for carrying artwork. A group of fifteen kids with two adults in tow, ascended the steps of the Art Institute. Several young couples walked hand in hand up the steps. Various sets of tourists and art lovers marched in and out of the museum, none of them carrying dangerous weapons, wearing snarling faces, or approaching us as nefarious characters.

In the cab, I said, "North Clark Street just south of Diversey."

"Where are we going?" Brad asked.

"Safest place I know of in the city," I said. "No one would think to look for us there."

The Womb was the sleaziest bar in the city. It was on Clark Street south of Diversey, across from the post office. The bar was in the basement of a crumbling building. The color scheme, which had changed numerous times over the years, had been returned to lurid tints, generally suggesting walls spray-painted with vomit. The entertainment used to be lesbians strippers in leather. Now dancing boys performed in skimpy outfits. They alternately gyrated slender hips on a tiny stage to the rear of the bar, or circumnavigated the central well, shaking down customers for tips. The joint had a grisly reputation for prostitution, somewhat of a higher-class notoriety for transvestites, transsexuals, and other transgender folks, plus it had underground nationwide fame for its after-hours parties, rumored to be filled with vast quantities of illegal drugs, gallons of booze, and lack of clothes on the partygoers. It matched our hotel as one of the last places I could think of that anyone would look for us.

I knew it would be open because they served a daily brunch. It was a lavish spread with over fifty different kinds of salads, cold pasta dishes, a plethora of meats, fruits, and vegetables. You could get omelets, waffles, and pancakes freshly made to your order, after which you could indulge in an enormous variety of desserts heavily weighted on the chocolate end of the spectrum.

It was just after noon when we walked in. The first bartender I saw was dressed in a purple, pure silk, full shirt with double pleats in back and very full long sleeves. He had on black gym shoes with bright yellow socks and black 2(X)IST boxer briefs. He was among the more conservatively dressed of the staff. The cook at the omelet table wore a red chef's hat and a single black strap of cotton around his neck which tapered down and connected to a contoured pouch. He also wore a carnation behind one ear. Both these guys had lean muscular figures that looked terrific in their outfits. The Monday noon crowd filled half the place.

When we were two feet inside the front door, Brad said, "What is this place?"

"A haven," I said.

We asked for and received a seat at a booth near the back. Moments later, our waiter appeared in sheer Silvery Short and Robe. He gave us some tips on specials, flirted with the three of us shamelessly, and sashayed away.

Brad shook his head. "Is this a gay bar?" he asked.

I glanced around. "It's more of a hallucination," I said, "but it grows on you."

As we perused the buffet table, the dancing boy left the stage at the far end of the room and pranced over to us. He seemed aptly dressed in a gold-banded thong. Another few beers, and his figure would no longer be appropriate for this outfit. Maybe they only had the second-string guys gyrating at Monday lunch. Brad made shooing motions at the dancer, but I knew the drill. I stuck a buck in his pouch, and he left us alone.

I picked up a broccoli-and-cheese omelet and a Caesar salad, along with some onion soup. Scott found the appetizer/finger food that he liked so much and loaded up. Brad stuck to waffles.

After I'd consumed enough to take the edge off my hunger, I said, "We've got big problems. Brad, you said you were scared and Glen had made some kind of deal. What's going on?"

We spoke in soft voices, although the size of the booths, the distance we were from any other patron, and the sounds of music for the dancers wafting over hidden speakers were sufficient to mute anything we said.

"How can I be sure I can trust you?" Brad asked.

Scott said, "We can't be sure we can trust you, either. We've been shot at. You're scared. Who are you planning to turn to, if not us?"

Brad's immediate response was to wolf down huge quantities of waffle while glancing anxiously around the room.

A Nick Bakes poster on the wall next to the booth was of a young blond lying in bed with his pajama tops open, and the bottoms unbuttoned enough to reveal white briefs. I always thought it looked like Scott when we first met. I think he's even more beautiful now.

Scott broke the silence. "We've got no choice but to trust each other." He explained that the police didn't believe us about Glen's death.

Brad finished his waffle and took several enormous gulps of coffee. Immediately the waiter appeared and re-filled the mug. He rested a hand on Brad's shoulder and leaned a hip more than companionably close. He finished his onerous duty and sauntered off.

"I don't know if I can take this place," Brad said.

"We could all be dead if we don't do something," I said. "We've got to know what the hell was going on. You've got that information. Like Scott said, who are you going to turn to?"

"I don't know," Brad said. "We were down there together. We didn't plan for it to happen."

"What?" I demanded.

Brad mumbled, "Drugs."

"I knew it," I said. It was such a stupid cliché thing for Glen Proctor to involve himself in: illegal drug trafficking. He double-crossed somebody and got himself killed.

"What kind of drugs?" I asked almost bored.

"Not *kinds* of drugs," Brad said. "Drug *people*. We had a line on where Frederico Torres was hiding."

Everybody knew from the headlines that Frederico Torres was the most powerful drug kingpin in Mexico. Huge numbers of police officials in twelve countries and millions of dollars had been spent hunting for him. He had eluded numerous police dragnets and was wanted by the authorities in half the countries in the world not only for illegal substances but for his involvement in assassination and gunrunning as well.

"He's got a price of seven million dollars on his head," Brad said. "Glen found out where he was and was determined to cash in. He'd lost all the money he made in baseball. This was his way of showing his dad he could make it on his own and that he'd kicked his drug habit for good and was making up for it. He knew where Frederico was. I was going to help Glen turn him in. We were going to split the money, but something went wrong near Huautla, in Mexico."

"Why didn't you just call the police?" I asked.

"We were going to, but we didn't know which cops to trust. Glen suggested we give the information to cops in this country. He decided we should split up. He came a day ahead. I think he had a meeting with somebody at the airport in Acapulco, but he wouldn't tell me. He gave me a number to call when I got here, which I guess was you guys. I flew out of Mexico City to Ciudad Victoria."

Brad wiped his palm across his brow. I didn't think his nervousness was from being turned on by the dancing boy, the hired help, or the decor.

"On the way to Mexico City, I drove by the place where twenty-four Mexicans were killed in an ambush. There's a lot of drug traffic through that region. I think I was lucky to get out of there alive. I knew I shouldn't have gotten involved with Glen. He always had the goofiest schemes."

"Are you sure he wasn't trying to smuggle drugs?" I asked.

Brad looked down at the table, pawed at his hair again, and looked sideways at us. "He wasn't. I went through his luggage and my own, in case he tried to stuff some in that I didn't know about."

"You knew him pretty well," Scott said.

"I know I'm not bright, but I've been around enough to recognize Glen's type."

"How'd you get involved with him?" I asked.

"I was in Ciudad Victoria doing some preparation for the winter baseball leagues. I'm a sort of coach and player. It's the only place I can still play. Nobody else wants me. My knee's a little gimpy from an operation. Glen came through a few weeks ago. He suggested a vacation together. It was nice seeing a guy I could talk to and understand. I'm not prejudiced, you understand, but at least he spoke English. Besides, Glen always was a good guy to party with."

"How'd he stumble onto this drug lord's whereabouts?" I asked.

"I'm not sure," Brad said. "Glen didn't explain much to me. He just wanted my help."

"Did he know before he ran into you?" I asked.

Brad thought a minute. "I don't think so. He didn't start talking about it until the day we left Cuernavaca for Acapulco. That was five days ago."

"Why did he need your help?" I asked.

"I'm not sure. I think I was supposed to be like sort of a bodyguard.

"You have no idea what happened?" I asked.

"Only a little. I know he was sending the information about the drug guy's whereabouts here and not bringing it with him. I got nervous and figured I'd better get out of the country for a while. At the Mexico City airport, I thought I was being followed. I had a scheduled stop in Ciudad Victoria. While there, I checked in at my place to pick up a few things. My neighbor told me that some mean-looking dudes were looking for me. At the airport gate I saw the guy who I thought was following me in Mexico City. I don't think he saw me. I turned around and left. A friend agreed to drive me as far as Brownsville, Texas. I just wanted to get back to the United States as quick as I could and get hold of Glen. Brownsville is where I saw the bus I would have been on boarded by guys with guns."

The waiter returned and sidled up to our booth. His thong came up to about the edge of our table. In an incredibly deep bass voice, he asked, "Is everything satisfactory?"

Brad said, "Get the hell out of here, faggot!"

The young man drew himself up to his full-fairied fury. I forestalled a confrontation. Much as the young man didn't deserve to be treated harshly, I wasn't in the mood for confrontation. I echoed Brad's sentiments, but with a more friendly dollar bill tucked into his G-string and a pat on the ass.

To Brad I said, "Keep your homophobia to yourself. If you're going to get out of this, it's going to be because of us."

"I should call the cops," Brad said. "I don't even know what homophobia is."

"Call them," I said.

Brad hesitated. He went through his head-scratching routine again. "I could tell them I think Frederico Torres is after me and that his men killed Glen."

"What proof are you going to give them?" I asked.

"That they killed Glen."

"We have no body and no proof for that," I said.

"But they attacked you."

"And you don't like us, so you're going to call the police and use an attack on us as a way to get protection for yourself. Does that really make sense to you? Do you think they'll buy your story?"

"They have to," Brad said. "Don't they?"

"Your trust in the local constabulary is quaint but misguided," I said.

"They can't just come into this country and kill people," Brad said. "We've got laws against that."

I was polite enough not to laugh at him. Now that we had information from him about who was probably chasing Glen, I wasn't sure how much good he was to us. I didn't want this homophobic creep hanging around, who we might have to protect or save. I also wasn't sure what we could do with the information.

I wanted to shower and shave, meet with Mrs. Proctor, talk with my lawyer, and be safe in my own home. The immediate questions were how to be safe and how to handle Brad. I could easily see him getting himself killed by doing something stupid.

"Homophobic means I don't like gay people," Brad said apropos of nothing.

Scott nodded.

Brad shook his head. "I just don't like being in this place," Brad said. "I'm liberal. In bars in the minor leagues, I even met a few guys who I let give me blowjobs. Doesn't mean I'm gay or that I hate you guys. Just this place gives me the creeps."

I glanced around. To someone unaccustomed to the more flamboyant side of gay life, it could be a little difficult to take. The atmosphere was like the most outrageous parts of the Pride Parade, the ones they usually show on television, or on hate videos put out by the religious right.

Scott said, "We should call Todd again."

So I did. His answering service told me to hold on. He must have left a message to page him immediately if we called.

After I explained everything to him, Todd said, "Does Brad know where Frederico is?"

"I don't know," I said. "We never asked him."

"You don't want to know," Todd said. "Don't let him tell you the place. He's got to get himself to the authorities immediately. Go from where you are to the nearest police station and stay there no matter what. That's the Twenty-third District at Halsted and Addison. I will bring reinforcements."

"What did you find out about old man Proctor's business?" I asked.

"No time now. Immediately get him to the police station."

I walked back to the table. Brad wasn't there.

"In the john," Scott answered my unspoken question.

"He didn't want an escort?" I asked.

"He said he could handle it."

I motioned for our waiter, who came over, leaned up next to me, and whispered in my ear, "I'd love to take you home if neither of these guys is your lover."

"Thanks, I'm spoken for," I said.

Scott hadn't been recognized by anyone in the bar, or if he had, they'd kept a discreet distance. Going out with him can be a hellish experience. Get one fan who recognizes him, and you could have a maelstrom of screaming lunatics around you in seconds. Other times he manages to slip by completely unrecognized. Last year he dragged me to the Chicago Auto Show, the biggest one in the country. We'd walked around for two hours, and he was completely unrecognized.

I paid the check and sat on the edge of the booth to wait for Brad. The dancing boy was immediately upon me. I had sat spread-legged with both knees jutting into the aisle. He chose to deposit himself on my right knee and proceeded to make his pouch jump and jiggle on my thigh.

For my dollar, I got a hug and a whispered "Thank you." He smiled and moved on to his next victim.

"It's so nice they're friendly," Scott said.

"Hell of a way to make a living," I said. "I wonder if they have real jobs."

"Ask them sometime," Scott said.

"I'm not sure I care that much."

"Brad's taking a long time," Scott said.

I leaned out of the booth and looked toward the back and the washrooms. "I hope he didn't get lost or molested," I said.

"I'm going to check," Scott said.

I scanned the crowd. A tall, beefy guy and a short, thin guy with a wispy mustache lounged near the door. Undercover cops or . . . I began to feel uneasy.

A moment later, Scott hurried up to our table. "He's gone," Scott announced.

"What do you mean, gone? He can't be gone!"

"I mean gone, as in 'no longer at this place in this universe,' " Scott said.

I needed sarcasm at this moment. I nodded discreetly in the direction of the suspicious guys near the front. "Did Brad see them?"

"I don't know when they came in."

"Come on," I said. We both rushed to the back together. We checked both johns. Empty. A third door led off from the hallway with the washrooms. I pushed it open. The room was set up like a hundred dressing rooms in tawdry theaters. A mirror with a row of lights around the perimeter. Cramped quarters with clothes strewn everywhere. Racks of clothes against the walls. A dancing boy sat in a tatty flannel bathrobe. A cigarette dangled from his lips while he perused a textbook whose title read *Sociology of Groups in the Wild.*

He glanced up at us. "You're not supposed to be back here, but for you, I'll make an exception. I charge extra for two at the same time."

"We're looking for the guy who was sitting with us," I said. "Kind of a big beefy guy. Did he come through here?"

The dancer drew his robe closer around himself. "I remember him. Haven't seen him, but I've been on break only a couple minutes. You'll have to ask Charley."

"Where's he?" I asked.

The dancer nodded his head toward another door farther back. Through this we strode. This room was maybe eight-by-eight with a large metal desk in the middle, three filing cabinets against the far wall, and a door to our right.

A fat man smoking a cigar gave us a brief glance. He wore a T-shirt with holes in it. A ledger book was open in front of him. He wrote several figures into it, then raised an eyebrow in our direction.

"I got a license," he said. "Or if you aren't the cops or the city inspector, I don't provide the dancing boys for prostitution. I run a clean place here. I can't get you any favors."

"Did a big guy with greased-down hair go through here a few minutes ago?" I asked.

"Nope. I'm busy. You don't belong here. Leave."

I marched over and opened the far door.

"Hey, what do you think you're doing?" The fat guy lumbered over.

I ignored him and peered out into an alley. I saw no sign of Brad. The fat man grabbed my arm. I shook him off and said, "Is there any other way out of here?"

"Fuck off, buddy!"

Obviously he wasn't going to win Miss Congeniality of this alley.

I looked over my shoulder at Scott. "You sure he didn't go out the front?"

"Positive," he said.

"Get out of here!" the fat guy roared.

"Okay," I said. We walked out the back door.

6

To our right, the backs of buildings extended twenty feet and ended in a chain-link gate which prevented egress in that direction. To the left the alley twisted and curved toward Wrightwood Avenue. Because it had only one exit, the alley was unfrequented.

"I don't like this place," Scott said.

"We'll hurry."

The gray and chill of the day before had returned on a rising northeast breeze. The mid-October afternoon gave a grim forewarning of an unpleasant winter.

I zipped the jacket Lester had brought me and pulled the collar closer around me.

The buildings surrounding the alley presented bleak, soot-encrusted faces toward us and cast elaborate shadows that made the alley seem even cooler and more sinister than it needed to be. I wished I had a heavier coat. At the last curve before Wrightwood, Scott grabbed my arm and pointed. I saw a row of behemoth-sized plastic garbage cans. In the gathered shadows behind them at ground level, I saw a hint of blue fabric.

Scott hurried over and moved one of the containers. Behind it was Brad. Together we stooped over him. He was on his back. I saw blood seeping from a wound above his left ear. The seam on the right sleeve of his jacket had been ripped open.

"How bad is it?" Scott asked.

"Let's get those two fags!" a voice called.

I looked up to see five guys who all looked to be in their mid to late teens approaching us from the Wrightwood Avenue end of the alley. It is far too common for gangs of young straight guys to come into gay neighborhoods, hang around, and wait for gay people to beat up. These guys must have known the exit for the Womb, that the alley was rarely used and waited for victims.

I stood up and faced them. I felt powerful and invulnerable as adrenaline rushed through me. I didn't see any weapons. I knew that Scott and I could take care of any five unarmed teenagers.

"Let's take them," I said.

Scott yelled, "Fire!"

The five teenagers gave him an odd look. They took a couple of paces forward. Scott continued to bellow. Scott's response was certainly one of the ones that was highly recommended by police departments.

A scrawny bepimpled kid, the shortest one of them with the scraggliest hair said, "Nobody's going to hear them. It's a bluff. We can take them."

Nevertheless, three of them hesitated.

Scott tried shouting "fire" again, but no people appeared at any of the dirt begrimed windows or at the dilapidated and padlocked doors.

"Ain't nobody but us and the fags," said the skinny kid. He came forward with the confidence that his buddies would follow.

I decided not to wait for rescue or for them to make a concerted move. I launched myself toward the biggest one—maybe as tall as me, but at least fifty pounds heavier. He went into a defensive crouch. At the last second, I pivoted to the right away from him and slapped the palm of my hand up and into the bridge of the skinny kid's nose. He collapsed to the ground. One of them grabbed me from behind. I lifted my right foot and brought the heel back sharply against his shin. He let go. The big one tried to grab me in a bear hug. As he reached, I sent my hand darting for a grasp at his genitals. I connected with soft folds of the front of his jeans and a significant portion of his dick and balls. I did my best to crush them in my grip. He screamed and fell to his knees.

Scott had the wrist of one of the others, held up against the kid's back almost to the neck. The fifth one ran off.

The wailing of fire-truck sirens made a delicious noise. Someone *had* been listening. The firemen called the cops. When they arrived, I told them for sure we wanted to press charges. They took the kids away. The official constabulary was impressed that one of the guys having been attacked was Scott Carpenter the famous baseball player, but seemed a trifle confused when he and I insisted that it was a hate crime—gay-bashing—and not just an ordinary mugging.

An older cop with grizzled white hair and a limp took down all the information. He wanted us to take Brad to a hospital. Soon after the arrival of all the official personages, Brad sat up. He claimed he didn't want assistance. I wanted him at the police station as soon as possible. It might be going over the police radio about the identity of the mugging victim as a well-known baseball player. That could alert all kinds of people, some of whom were not out to act in our best interest.

"Why'd you run out on us?" I asked at one point while the police were busy loading teenagers into the squadrol, Chicago's version of what in an old gangster movie would have been called a paddy wagon.

Brad shrugged. "I thought I recognized two guys who walked in," he said. "I panicked. I've never been stuck like this. Glen's dead. I'm really scared. I was afraid to trust you guys. I thought you might sell me out."

"To whom? For what?" I asked.

He scratched his head again. If I saw that gesture a whole lot more times, I'd shave his head bald myself.

We drove to the police station in a blue-and-white cop car. Scott and I sat in the backseat and Brad up front next to a cop, who was more than delighted to ignore the gay aspects of what had occurred and concentrate on the fact that he had an all-star pitcher in the back of his car. We talked baseball for the mercifully short trip to the station.

My lawyer met us at the admitting desk. Todd shooed away all the solicitous and inquiring cops, and asked for and got a private room to talk to us.

"What the hell is going on?" he asked when we were finally alone.

I told him the story while Scott and Brad slumped in gray metal folding chairs, in a gray-walled room, with a painted gray wooden table.

Todd was tall and waspishly thin. His charcoal trousers were held up by black suspenders, stretched over a white shirt. He wore a perfectly knotted tie. He'd spread his gray suit coat over a chair. I'd only ever seen him dressed as if for court. If I asked him about his attire, I knew he'd say that for a trip to the police station, it never hurt to look one's best. It might be impressive at the right moment.

He wore glasses with thin gold rims. His sunken cheeks and crinkles around his eyes added to the impression he gave everyone that, with a few minor alterations, he could have been anyone's maiden aunt. He often sounded like it, too.

After I finished my story, he thought for several minutes, then said, "I'll be right back."

He returned in five minutes with two uniformed cops who escorted Brad out.

"I need to talk to you guys alone," Todd said after they left the room.

"Brad might try to run," I said.

"I called in a favor," Todd said. "The commander of the police district and I have worked together before. Throwing Scott's name around didn't hurt. Those two guys will keep him safe."

Todd rested his skinny butt on the top of the table. I stood near the door. Scott remained in the chair.

"What have you found out?" I asked.

"Several bits of information," Todd said. "First, old man Proctor is generally regarded as an honest real-estate dealer. No known shady connections. As Lester said last night, Mrs. Proctor's in the same business as her sort of ex-husband and the two of them are incredible rivals."

"Like Blake and Alexis on *Dynasty,*" I said.

Todd frowned. He didn't approve of popular culture. In music he preferred Gregorian chant. Anything tuneful later than 1899 was anathema to him. He on occasion deigned to watch a silent movie but hadn't been to a talking movie since his freshman year of high school. He spent his free moments rereading Samuel Richardson or all thirty-two of Sir Walter Scott's novels in the order they were published.

"It's a classic case of two separated people into each other viciously and irrevocably," Todd said. "I found out that before their marriage they were competitors. My source says that it was a strange union. In the early years of the marriage, Mr. Proctor hired a gigolo to catch her in a compromising position. Meanwhile, she hired a prostitute to do the same to him. In this case, a picture might be worth a thousand words, but it could also be worth millions of bucks. Eventually, they wound up trading pictures, realized what they'd done, and had a secret meeting in Hong Kong to try and make peace."

"How'd you find out all this stuff?" I asked.

"My accountant is the smartest lesbian on this continent. She knows an enormous number of secrets about rich people. I have her looking into both Proctors' dealings for illegality of any kind. If it's there to be found, she'll find it."

Todd took off his glasses, pulled out a handkerchief, and polished his lenses. When he had them settled back on his

105

nose, he continued, "They discovered they'd turned each other on with their aggressiveness. Sort of fellow cut-throats. Piranhas in bed with each other. For a few years they tried to stay apart, but the attraction between them remained incredibly powerful."

"Sounds nuts," Scott said.

"People get turned on by some odd things," Todd said. "They ended up getting married and even had kids, Glen and Bill. The marriage didn't really put an end to their competition. Eventually they dueled for their kids' affection. For a couple of years, they holed up in separate wings of that big mansion up in Lake Forest."

"What ended the marriage?" I asked.

"They aren't divorced. That's why I said sort of ex-husband. They're separated. Haven't lived together in five years."

"Why not divorce and be done with it?" Scott asked.

"Who knows?" Todd said. "Business? A sick attraction? Power? Could be anything. Reportedly, they would do anything to hurt each other in business."

"Nuts!" Scott said.

"That may be," Todd said. "What I also found out is that they were both interested in several large deals down in Mexico lately especially with the North American Free Trade Agreement that was signed recently. My source says that the son, Glen, was sent down by Daddy to do some work for him, although it wasn't clear whether it was licit or illicit work. As an older son, Glen supposedly was quite a disappointment to his father."

"I don't suppose he dreamed about having a drug-addict, has-been baseball player for a kid," I said.

"Not a dream come true," Todd agreed.

"So how does that affect us?" Scott asked.

"I'm not sure," Todd said. "The kid comes back from Mexico and says he is in trouble and does not run home to Mommy or Daddy. I would think they've got enough money to cover up almost anything."

"Enough cash to buy off an unhappy South American drug lord?" I asked.

Todd shrugged. "From the way you describe Glen Proctor, he seemed to be living out some Terry and the Pirates fantasy."

"Maybe he was just trying to win his parents' love and affection," Scott said.

"You have an invitation to talk to Mrs. Proctor?" Todd asked.

I nodded.

"Then go talk to her. She might know something that will help. The people after you have to be placated. I'm not sure how you go about doing that."

We discussed that for half an hour but got nowhere.

The old cop with the limp came in and said, "We got a mob of reporters out here, want to talk to Mr. Carpenter about what's going on."

"You going to hide it was a gay-bashing?" Todd asked Scott.

"No," Scott said. "But I'm not sure I want to talk to them now."

"Whoever's after us has probably heard where we are," I said.

Todd agreed.

We left the room. The cop limped over and pointed out the window. "Minicams are here."

I glanced out at the crowd of milling reporters. I saw a few I recognized from the ten o'clock news on different stations. I also saw several people in the ubiquitous charcoal gray suits I had come to associate with those people after us. If they were minions of South American drug dealers, they did not fit the cliché look as presented on so many American television shows. They looked neat, clean, and respectable. I didn't see the big guy with the blond mustache and bald head.

"I can get you out the back," our cop buddy said and left to arrange it.

"Can we get police protection?" Scott asked.

"Probably not," Todd said.

"We should hire personal bodyguards," Scott said.

"I've already taken care of it," Todd said. "Guards may simply draw attention to you, but we've got to at least try."

"You trust these guys?" Scott asked.

"I've used this company before," Todd said. "When I called today, I didn't say who they'd be protecting. They have no way of knowing that I'm your personal lawyer. I trust them. Protection is only a temporary solution. If these people want to kill you, they will. You've got to try to find them so you can negotiate. You've got to find out how Glen managed to connect you with what he was into, and what to give these guys to make them go away. I do not have high hopes."

"You mean we're dead already?" Scott asked.

"I'm not going to start lying to you now," Todd said. "I've always told you the truth before. You are not in a good position."

"I could make a statement on television," Scott said. "I'm well known enough that the media would let me talk."

Todd considered this for a few moments. Finally he said, "Let me try to work out some kind of announcement. Although a plea to a drug lord for understanding sounds kind of iffy to me."

I was forced to agree.

"We've got to get out of here and someplace safe," Scott said.

"I want to talk to Mrs. Proctor," I said.

"Yes, that has to be done," Todd agreed. "Let's get the cop to get us out of here. The longer that crowd mingles in front, the less comfortable I am."

Todd left the room and a minute later returned with our cop buddy. Out in the hall two guys who'd been sitting in the plastic folding chairs near the front desk when we came in got up. I'd assumed they were criminals in a drug bust. They had long, stringy hair of an indeterminate brown shade. One guy had his pulled back in a ponytail. He looked like he had a slight paunch. The other was scrawny and had the deep scars and red residue of violent acne all over his early twenties face. I didn't see a gun visible on either one of them, but they wore sweaters and jackets under which they could have been concealed. Todd introduced them as our protection.

I pulled Todd aside. "These guys are guards?"

"The best," Todd assured me.

We gathered Brad and our little group trudged down a gray corridor around a bend and into an interior garage. At the door I asked, "Where's Brad?"

Todd hurried back the way we came. He returned in a minute with a look of concern on his face. "Two guys claiming to be his lawyers came to see him. Cops let them talk to him." Todd shook his head. "They're all gone now. Nobody saw them go. Let's get out of here."

The cop piled us into a squadrol. We drove out of the parking lot onto Addison, west past Wrigley Field, and north up Clark Street. We stopped at Irving Park and Clark and got out. The cop got an autograph from Scott, gave us a cheery wave, and left.

"I'll do more searching," Todd said. "Be careful. Those two guys are good, but don't take any chances."

Our guards waited a discreet distance away. Todd hailed a cab and left. The two derelict-looking guards sidled up to us.

"You guys have a car?" I asked.

The one with the ponytail nodded.

"You have names?" Scott asked.

Ponytail's brown eyes stared into Scott's for several uncomfortable moments, then he pointed to himself and said, "Bernie," and then pointed to his buddy and said, "Angelo."

They made no fuss or mention about Scott's being famous. I found this refreshing and disconcerting. Their car was a 1975 Chevrolet with the tail pipe dangling down in back, a pair of dice hanging from the rearview mirror, and a statue of St. Christopher on the dashboard. None of this was tremendously reassuring in terms of expecting great protection from these guys, but I knew Todd would hire only the best.

Scott and I piled into the back. In front Angelo shoved his seat all the way back, scrunching into my knees. He propped his feet up on the dashboard, pulled out a toothpick, and proceeded to clean his teeth.

I gave Bernie the address Mrs. Proctor had given us. Bernie drove with the élan and aggressiveness of a mad cabbie.

On a late Monday afternoon the traffic on Lake Shore Drive through the Loop to the Near West Side of Chicago was fairly heavy. Even though school kids got out for Columbus Day, most people had to work. A lot of the Near West Side had burned down after the Martin Luther King assassination in 1968. For years most of it hadn't come back, and much of it was vacant lots and old factories. Over time the westward expansion of the Loop had begun to reinvigorate the area. Presidential Towers was one of the big developments, along with Oprah Winfrey's Harpo Studios. Others had followed and now some of the area had trendy restaurants and old factories, and warehouses converted to upscale condos.

We followed Lake Street west under the El tracks. The slatted track and the rusting metal above made for a gloomy corridor down the still-unrenovated portion of this end of the Near West Side.

On the south side of Lake Street, between Elizabeth and Racine streets was a block-long warehouse, five stories tall built of dirty maroon brick, and occupying the entire block. The address we had directed us to Willard Court, little more than an alley which bisected the entire block and the warehouse. Both sides of Lake Street were filled with cars. After working hours, this area cleared out quickly. A few blocks earlier, the streets had been nearly vacant. Here cars crowded nose to nose, but few places seemed around to justify their existence. No marquees for a trendy restaurant appeared.

We halted at the entrance to Willard Court. I could see that it was actually a cul-de-sac with several black limousines parked amid a plethora of semitrailer trucks. No one seemed to be bustling around at this time on a Monday afternoon, but it was inside Willard Court that we had been directed to go.

Bernie bobbed his ponytail in the direction of the glorified alley. "You sure about this?" he asked.

I looked at the address again. "Yeah," I said. "Doesn't look too promising."

"I don't know," Scott said.

"We'll go in with you," Angelo said. He took his feet off the dashboard, reached behind his back, and pulled out a gun. He checked to see that it was loaded, then shoved it back in the hidden holster.

Bernie nosed the car into the entrance to Willard Court. He almost ran over one of the denizens indigenous to Lake Street and the Near West Side. The cops on the street called them he/shes. The rest of us called them transvestite prostitutes. They, along with their sisters and a rare brother, plied their trade along the dark depths beneath the El tracks. She tapped the hood of the car with a gloved hand, winked at us, and swayed away on her spike heels.

Angelo made no attempt to park, but pulled twenty feet inside and let the car idle. Here our perception of the alley changed dramatically. Recessed into the wall on the left and running for twenty feet was a plate-glass window. Through it we could see brightly lit, plant-strewn elegance.

A woman in black pants, white shirt, and black tie with a black-and-white patch on her shoulder that said security marched up to the car. At least she didn't brandish a weapon. On the other hand, we didn't get a smile and a welcome.

She motioned for Angelo to roll down the window.

111

"Here to see Mrs. Proctor," I said from the backseat.

She pulled a radio from her belt, stepped a few feet away from the car, pushed a button, and spoke. Moments later, she came back and asked our names.

After I told her, she murmured into the radio. A moment later she nodded.

"You can't park here," she said. "Mason and Carpenter are expected."

"You want to go in by yourself?" Bernie asked.

"No," Scott said.

"I need some guarantee of our safety," I said.

She gave me an odd look. "You can't park here because you need a special permit. You have a special permit?"

Heads shook.

"Then you have to move."

"We need some kind of guarantee," I repeated.

"You can leave if you want," she said. "If you want to see Mrs. Proctor, you'll have to move the car off the premises and come back." She didn't sound mean and nasty, just like a bureaucrat insisting that her orders be obeyed.

She seemed in no rush to hurry us off, nor did I think she would change her mind anytime in this or the next century.

"Park the car, Bernie," I said. "I want to talk to her. You can come in with us."

Bernie backed the car out and found a space on Elizabeth Street a half block from the warehouse. We walked back to the entrance with them. We passed another of the he/shes, this one in a short leather red dress and pink shawl draped around her shoulders. Barely enough against the mild October chill.

Back inside I saw that Willard Court, whether alley, street, or redeemed cul-de-sac, was spotless. For all the trucks and the incumbent garbage that must emanate from them, not a scrap of paper was out of place. Someone must sweep the alley several times a day.

The windows above the shadowed alley all seemed

opaque and featureless, like any other abandoned warehouse. But none of these were broken out.

Inside the entrance, I saw two other security guards besides the woman we had already met. They were all excessively polite as they escorted us deeper into the building.

We ascended stairs of naked wood, newly constructed and unvarnished. I caught the whiff of fresh pine. We entered a room containing banks of television screens. A lone guard nodded at our escort. Two of the guards with us sat down at stations and immediately commenced a security check with the first. We were ignored.

The guard who had accosted us in the alley led us across the room.

"Good security system," I said.

"You need it these days and in this neighborhood," she said. "It may be upscale, but it isn't the safest yet."

The fourth side of the room was completely glass. It extended up two stories and looked out on an English-garden landscape. We walked through a sliding glass door. I saw that this atrium extended up five stories to a skylight that stretched the entire width of the building, as did the garden. The hedges were trimmed perfectly, flowers bloomed in riotous abundance, and a brook flowed from a small waterfall from our right to out of sight on our left. The fragrance was an early June meadow along a pristine stream. Someone had invested a huge amount of money in making the interior of this relic of a building an oasis of refinement.

The guard led us through a series of paths to an elevator. She rode up with us to the fifth floor.

The doors opened to a marble floor that covered an office that must have encompassed a quarter of the entire floor. Two rows of sleek steel and aluminum desks sat in front of us. Most seemed to have computers and plants prominently displayed on their tops. To our left and right, huge rubber trees in enormous pots flanked the entrance.

Just beyond them on each side were paintings by René Magritte, an odd surrealistic touch in this modern office.

Except for the humming of neon lights and the whir of what I presumed was the heating system, there wasn't a sound.

The guard prodded our elbows gently, and we followed her through a door at the far side of the room. We entered a twenty-by-twenty-foot room. Against the old brick wall on the far end, rows of plants nearly engulfed a teak desk at which a woman sat.

Mrs. Proctor wore her hair cut straight to the sides, almost shoulder length, with nary a curl. Flecks of gray peeked from among the light brown. I doubted if she colored her hair. She wore a Tahari beige silk sarong jacket and trousers and matching Nine West shoes. She rose from the desk. The guard left. Mrs. Proctor met us halfway across the room.

She led us to a small seating area of low-slung black leather chairs and couch with a chrome coffee table in between. The gray light of October seeped through a skylight directly above us. After we were seated, she asked if we wanted refreshments. We both said no.

Bernie and Angelo stood against the door.

Mrs. Proctor nodded in their direction. "You need bodyguards?"

I said, "After we explain, you'll understand."

She nodded, then said, "I've been trying to get back to you since you phoned. Something is wrong."

"Mrs. Proctor," I said, feeling awful to be the one telling a mother that her son was dead. "Glen was staying with us. When we came in early yesterday morning"—I stopped and gulped. Telling Bill or Mr. Proctor had not made this moment any easier—"we found him dead."

She rose slowly to her feet. Her eyes never left mine.

"I'm sorry," I said.

She seemed to totter. Scott jumped up and rushed to her

side. She leaned heavily on his arm. She covered her face with one hand.

"Please," she said. "Please. This can't be true. He was . . . I want to . . . He's in . . . He's supposed to be"—she moved her hand away from her face—"this can't be true."

"I saw him," I said. "I touched him. I wish it weren't true."

"Why haven't the police called? What is going on?"

She sat back down. Scott stayed next to her. Mrs. Proctor's hand trembled as she pointed at me. "Tell me what happened."

I told her the story from the beginning. I left out a great deal about the tunnels, figuring she wasn't interested. When I described our reentry to the penthouse and finding the body gone, she rose to her feet.

She disdained Scott's proffered arm. "And what did my husband say yesterday when you told him?" she asked. She had enough cold in her voice to freeze all the moisture on the planet in seconds.

"He claimed we were wrong," I said.

She strode behind the couch and leaned against it. I have never seen a more self-possessed, more controlled, and more furious person.

"Oh, he'd say you're wrong because he'd know he'd somehow killed his son. If one of his idiotic schemes has gone haywire and it killed my son, I will not rest until every bone of my husband's body has endured pain." A tear started at the corner or her eye, but her voice did not waver. "I will break him. I will destroy him. All the devils in hell will not have suffered as much as my husband when I am through with him."

I didn't dare interrupt her spectacular diatribe. She pulled a lace hankie out of her jacket pocket and dabbed at her eyes and nose.

She said, "I loved Glen so much." Her fury spent, she now leaned against the back of the couch propping herself up with both hands. She lowered her head and shook it back and forth as she said over and over, "It can't be."

I had no idea what to say, so I said nothing.

When her voice had run down and she'd stood for some time in silence, I said, "Is there something we can get you? Someone we can call?"

She looked up at me and shook her head. "I want to sit down," she said. She matched the action to the words. Scott reseated himself in the chair next to me.

With her hands folded in her lap and her eyes shut, she breathed deeply for several minutes. Without opening her eyes, she said, "Tell me again what happened."

I did so, slowly and carefully, including what had happened to us since we found her son.

When I was finished, she spoke so quietly that we had to strain to listen.

"Glen was my favorite," she said. "I know mothers aren't supposed to have them, but I couldn't help it. He always wanted to be independent and free. Always had a mind of his own. Rebelled against being under his father's thumb, as I did against my father when I was a child." She sighed. "He had so many gifts. He could have been so many things."

I didn't add that something in his upbringing had contributed to his drinking and drug addiction, and that her little boy was hardly a saint. I suppose she knew that. I hesitated bringing up the drug lords. I wasn't sure who we could trust with what knowledge.

"We've been trying to find out what he was doing in Mexico," I said.

She looked startled. "Working for me."

"Mr. Proctor told us Glen was working for him."

"He couldn't have been," Mrs. Proctor said. "Glen had specific people to meet for me. Information to gather and on-site inspections to make."

"Do you have contacts down there who could give us information?" I asked.

"I have several business offices. What kind of information?"

"He must have been doing something down there that led to his being killed here."

"Possibly."

"Why Mexico?" Scott asked.

"Huge potential for growth," Mrs. Proctor said. "Lots of possibility for rapid expansion. We've got mall deals that would make anything in this country look like peanuts. It's practically virgin territory down there."

"Why send Glen?" I asked.

"Why not?" she countered.

I tried to phrase this delicately. "I never heard of him having the best head for business."

The edges around her lips almost pulled up in a smile. "I was always trying to find something for Glen to do. Anything that could give him a sense of worth. Distract him from his vices. I wanted to help him, give him a sense of responsibility."

Mr. Proctor had said nearly the same thing. Both seemed eager to help their son.

"Glen would never have worked for my husband," Mrs. Proctor said.

"Why not?" I asked.

"We were bitter rivals, and Glen took my side in the family disputes. He disliked his father and didn't trust him."

Her husband had given us no indication of this attitude, and what she said contradicted what Bill Proctor had told us. I wondered what the father's and brother's opinion on her comment would be.

"Why was there so much rivalry?" I asked.

She snorted. "Jason is a jerk, but a lucky jerk. He came from money, but my family is old money. Yes he's wealthy, but I've built an empire larger than his, and I didn't need his help. He hated my being richer than he, that I made better investments than he, that I was more respected

117

around the world than he ever could be. Our marriage was tempestuous, to say the least. The heights were wild, but ultimately we couldn't stand each other."

"And you used the kids as pawns in your rivalries," Scott said.

"How dare you say such a thing!" she exploded.

"Because you didn't really know your son at all. You're angry at your husband, but neither you nor he seem really worried that something happened to your son."

"How dare you!" she demanded.

"I was his friend," Scott said. "Which he needed very badly. We used to talk a lot when he was going through his suspensions. He wanted to succeed in baseball so badly, he told me, because his talent was something neither you nor your husband could touch. If Glen weren't dead, I'd feel sorry for you. You and your husband might not have pulled the trigger, but you helped drive him to his vices and his destruction."

Her icy cold was turned on us. "I don't have to listen to this."

"I don't care what you listen to," Scott said. "We're leaving."

He got up and walked toward the door. In silence we retraced our steps back to Willard Court. As we turned onto Elizabeth Street, I grabbed Bernie.

"Look," I said. I pointed at a car parked in front of ours. A nondescript gray sedan with two men in dark clothes sitting in front. "I think they were the ones out front of our hotel," I said.

Bernie and Angelo thrust us into a nearby doorway. They put their hands near their weapons and advanced carefully on the duo in the car, who continued to sit almost casually. Seconds later, two very confused and angry maintenance men from a nearby factory had their legs spread and hands on top of the hood of their car.

Meeting Scott Carpenter, famous baseball player, mollified them enough that they weren't going to press charges.

"I'm sorry," I said when we got back in the car. "I've gotten so paranoid."

"Forget it," Angelo said. "Better to be safe." They uttered no word of reproof.

"Where to?" Angelo asked.

"We've got a few belongings at that hotel," Scott said. "We can pick them up, and then, with you along, make it back to our place. Maybe we'll be safe with you there."

7

"That was a complete fiasco," I said as we drove to the hotel.

"Rivals for their kids' affections." Scott shook his head.

"Oedipus would have had a field day," I said.

As usual, we had a hell of a time finding a parking space around the hotel. On a Friday or Saturday night, you could drive around for hours before you found a space. At this hour on a Monday, the nearest illegal space was two blocks away. We took it.

The lobby of our demented hotel was filled that afternoon with what looked like a transvestite convention. The last time I'd seen so many hairy legs under dresses was in a bar in Istanbul five years ago. Strangest gay bar I'd ever been in.

On a table on one side of the lobby was a silver tea set with elegant blue china cups and real silverware. The crowd may have looked weird, but they murmured in low voices and sipped their beverages with as much propriety as you'd find at high tea with the queen of England.

Edna motioned us over. She wanted to know how much longer we planned to stay. We told her we'd settle the bill now.

"Convention in town?" I asked her.

"It's their day off. I give the boys a little late-afternoon buffet every Monday. Not the kind of thing to advertise in the paper, but they like it. Been doing it for years. Good for business."

Suddenly one of the party goers gave a muffled screech. I saw one of them in a slinky red dress fanning herself with a well-manicured hand. A man in leather pants led her over to the desk. "Mandy needs help," he said.

Mandy looked plaintively at Edna. Between comforting her and handling our checkout, Edna seemed to take forever.

During all this, Bernie and Angelo made no comment. They simply accompanied us to our room. I wanted to get our few possessions and get out. As I swung open the door to the room, I glanced back into the hall. An old man holding onto the arm of a young prostitute tottered down the hall. The four of us were in the room and I was closing the door when it burst out of my hand.

Bernie and Angelo had their guns half out, but the old man stood with two very unpleasant-looking black holes staring at us from two very large guns. His companion had a very lethal-looking machine gun pointing out of her satchel.

With a raspy voice, the old man said, "Drop your guns on the bed, gentlemen."

Our bodyguards might have taken on the old man, but the machine gun was another matter. They put them on the bed.

The woman wore a bright red dress, and she carried a black leather satchel over one shoulder. Her spiked heels must have been at least six inches high. When I looked closely at her face, I noted wisps of mustache.

I examined the man with the raspy voice. He had to be in his mid-seventies, with lush gray hair on the top of his head. In either hand he held a silencer-equipped gun pointed at the four of us.

Scott threw up. That the residue that hit the carpet did not disfigure it says a great deal about the state the floor covering was in. The guy with the machine gun moved out of the doorway to the bathroom. I tried to follow Scott inside, but the black hole at the end of the gun caught my movement and held me still. I heard Scott heave several more times. Then I heard the swirl of water. Scott emerged several moments later, looking very white. He sat on the floor.

"Who are you?" I asked.

"Are you going to kill us?" Scott asked. He had rested his head against the wall. His paleness had deepened to green at a few spots on his face. He shivered and began to sweat.

The old man pointed at Bernie and Angelo. "Tie them up." Minutes later our guards were bound in torn sheets from the bed.

"All done." I thought someone else had entered the room, but it was a deep male voice coming from the person wearing the red dress.

Our elder captor instructed us that we would leave the hotel, making no sudden moves. "If you attempt to escape," he said, "we will shoot you." I believed him.

Outside, the guy in the red dress, who fit right in with the gang in the lobby, disappeared around the corner to the alley running alongside the building. Moments later, he returned driving a Ford Taurus with rental plates on it.

The guy with the raspy voice directed us into the backseat of the car.

"Your friend is not well," the raspy voice said.

"You got that right," I said. "Are we going to be alive or dead?"

"Alive, probably." The old man looked back at us. He gave an almost-impish grin. If I'd had the gun he was pointing at us, I'd have shot him. We crossed Halsted Street and continued west. This was a quiet residential street through the up-and-trendy DePaul area.

"Who are you?" I asked again.

"I am Equelle Ramirez. This is my son Jose. We came to America to get our jewels back."

"The necklaces," I said.

"You know about them?" Jose said.

"Yeah," I said. "Why didn't you just ask? You're welcome to them."

"We weren't sure you had them," Jose said. He took off his hat and wig to reveal a brush haircut and flawlessly smooth skin.

"Not sure we had them," Scott croaked.

"Yeah," Jose said. "You haven't been the easiest people to locate, and we couldn't find Proctor."

"He's dead," I said.

"I thought as much," Equelle said.

Jose said, "We knew he was coming to see you. He'd bragged about knowing a Mr. Carpenter, the great baseball player, and said he would visit you first. This was before he took the necklaces or before we discovered them missing."

"It is my fault he knew about them," Equelle said. "I was careless when I was working on them. I am old. I had to come here to correct my mistake. Those necklaces were special-ordered and paid for already. We couldn't afford not to have them back."

"How did you find us?" I asked.

"We were in the crowd outside the police station. We guessed about a rear exit. Jose followed you. He called me after you entered the factory complex."

"You followed us from there?" Scott asked.

"Yes. Back at the hotel, we were fortunate to find a closer illegal parking spot than you. While you settled your bill, Jose importuned a costume from an unlucky young man. Then we simply followed you upstairs."

"If you didn't kill Glen, who did?"

"His killers came from my country. They are probably from Frederico Torres, since Glen told us he had information on him.

"Glen told you?" I asked.

"We've done business with his family for years. I remember him from when he was a child. The boy was a thief and a sneak even then. I never dreamed he'd steal from us. If that was Torres's crowd, and they got hold of you and the necklaces, we would never have gotten them back."

"Where are the necklaces?" Jose asked.

"Scott has one on," I said. "The other is at the penthouse."

"We will go there immediately to retrieve it," Equelle said.

"It will be guarded and watched," I said. "If not by the police, then certainly by those people who want to catch us. There have to be more people on the lookout. A smart person would have our place constantly under surveillance, assuming we'd have to come back sometime to get our stuff."

This gave them pause for a minute. It would be nice to believe that they would take what they wanted and let us go.

"You also need the key to the penthouse, and you've got to get past the guard," I said.

"Why did you think Glen would be dead?" Scott asked.

"He talked like a fool," Jose said. "He claimed he had a lead on a big drug shipment, but that he had the key to even more valuable riches in his hand. He claimed he knew something about drug safe houses in major cities in this country. Certainly there was one in Chicago. Who knows if what he found out was true or not? He also said he'd found the location of Frederico Torres and was negotiating to get the reward or trying to figure out a way to collect on the reward without the police of your country or mine getting it away from him."

"How did he find out?" I asked.

Jose shrugged. "There are those like Glen Proctor who seem to be able to stumble onto vast quantities of luck. They run con games on themselves, hoping the string of good fortune will renew itself constantly. They never understand when it runs thin. It is never their fault; and somehow, before they hit bottom, another miracle tum-

124

bles into their lap, until finally the miracle crushes them."

I was barely interested in their philosophizing, but extremely concerned about Scott, and the possibilities of our surviving this encounter.

"How did he know about you and your dealing in jewels?" I asked.

"His father and mother were both good customers," Equelle said. "Much of our business is legitimate, but there are risks, and occasionally problems arise. Glen brought several of our precious stones across the border over the years."

"We'll take the necklace Mr. Carpenter has," Jose said. He lifted the gun in our direction. "Now."

Scott reached behind his neck, unhooked the clasp, and handed over the gleaming bauble.

"Did he tell you how much this was worth?" Jose asked.

"I wasn't interested," I said.

"Half a million at least," Jose said.

"It can't be," Scott said. "Why would he give us such a valuable thing?" Some of the color had returned to his face.

"Perhaps because he would be making a great deal more from revealing the location of Mr. Torres," Equelle said. "He is a much-wanted man."

"Or maybe he was too stupid to realize their value," I said.

"You were not fond of Glen Proctor?" Jose asked.

"Not much," I said.

They spoke in Spanish between themselves for several minutes. Then Jose turned back to us. "We're going to your apartment." He began to don his wig. "You will give me the key. We will enter the lobby, go upstairs, and come back together."

"The doorman won't recognize you," I said.

Equelle said, "You will convince him it is safe. I will keep a gun trained at Mr. Carpenter's right temple. If there is a problem, I will kill him."

I had no doubt he would.

"But won't anyone watching see me and attempt to talk to me, or spot me and kill me?" I asked.

"Why are they chasing you?" Equelle asked.

"We don't know," I said. "Sometimes they've tried to shoot to kill. Sometimes just to capture us. It's totally nuts."

"Maybe they think Glen gave you the information," Jose said. "Did he?"

"No!"

Equelle said, "I don't know how badly they want you. They must think you know or have something."

"Why doesn't Torres just move?" Scott asked. "Why all this chasing around trying to kill Glen and us? If the big problem is hiding the guy, why not just move?"

"You'll have to ask them," Equelle said.

"I'd rather not," I said.

We drove in silence for a few minutes. Something had been bothering me about these two, and finally it dawned on me. "Neither one of you has much of an accent," I said.

"Would you feel more comfortable if we talked like ignorant peasants just learning English?"

Equelle found a parking space a half block away from the penthouse. Jose and I got out.

"I could get killed by the people chasing us," I said.

Equelle leaned over and spoke through the opened passenger side door. "That would create a further diversion for Jose to enter your penthouse and get the necklace. I mean no harm to you, Tom Mason, but I must have my jewelry. It is simply business, and in case you were thinking of alerting the police, Jose has a little device on his person that signals to a little device in my pocket that all is not well. If, for any reason, that goes off, your partner is dead."

The side street was devoid of passersby who might look suspiciously at Scott edging into the front seat of the rental car. Equelle held the gun in his left hand, away from Scott. He *would* be ambidextrous.

Jose adjusted his skirt, gave his wig a final pat, and we marched down the street. I had to admit he was good. His movements and mannerisms rivaled Jaye Davidson in *The Crying Game*.

The walk to the penthouse was pleasantly uneventful. I didn't know whether or not I was comforted by the fact that Jose had not removed the machine gun from the gigantic purse he carried.

I saw little point in thinking of ways to escape from Jose. One push of a button, and Scott would be dead. I desperately wanted Jose to succeed.

My legs wobbled a bit as we strode through the entryway. Howard saw me and his hand reached for the phone. Jose grabbed Howard's arm.

"You don't need to be calling anybody," Jose said and let the tip of his machine gun peep out of his purse.

Howard licked his lips and shook his head.

Jose smiled. He pointed at me. "You stay down here and keep an eye on Howard's arm. You might even ask him what he knows since he seemed so eager to call someone as soon as he saw you. If everything is not in order when I return, you two and Mr. Carpenter will die."

Jose turned on his spike heels and marched to the elevator.

"Who was that?" Howard asked.

"You let somebody into the penthouse Saturday," I said.

"No. Never."

"Who were you going to call just now?"

"A friend. No one you know."

"How did they get to you?" I asked. "You know they're trying to kill us. How could you turn us in?"

Howard drew himself up straight and glared to one side of my head. "I don't know what you're talking about," he said.

I couldn't get anything else out of him.

Jose returned moments later with an enormous smile on his face. He walked behind the counter, ripped out the phone, and then smashed the butt of his machine gun into the console. There was a small pffft, and the computer screens went blank. "I can kill you, too," Jose told Howard.

Howard held up his hands in the Old West pose of being arrested.

Then Jose put his arm through mine, and we walked out of the building comfortably linked together.

"You got it?" I asked.

"It was just where you said it would be. Lucky for you."

We strolled casually into the October early evening around the corner of the building, crossed the street, and sauntered toward the car, seemingly a man and woman connected against the early-winter chill. Walking toward us were two women, dressed in sensible Republican cloth coats open to reveal black skirts cut just below the knee. White blouses peeked out of beige V-neck sweaters.

We passed them when we were about two feet from the car door. I saw Scott begin to raise the door handle. Equelle's gun rose from the front seat.

"You've got to let us go," I said.

"That is up to my father," Jose said. He motioned with his purse for me to get in.

Equelle had his gun pointed at Scott's head, but I thought that if I got back in that car, both of us would be dead. They couldn't just shoot us here. While not crowded, cars were going past, and people were strolling about nearby. They'd have to take us somewhere to kill us.

"Get in!" Jose commanded when I hesitated.

I didn't want to see Scott's blood and brains scattered all over the pavement mixed with my own. The barrel of the machine gun poked over the edge of the purse into the small of my back as he held the door open.

"Could you help me, miss?" It was one of the women we'd just passed. She was tugging at the edge of Jose's

128

purse. The woman must have been in her late forties or early fifties. Her companion was about five feet behind her, looking bewildered and lost.

"We just had a drink over on Rush Street, and we're trying to get back to Oak Street, but we must have turned the wrong way."

"Get out of here, lady," Jose said.

The other woman came close. "Is that a gun?" she asked pointing into the interior of the car.

Equelle lowered the gun for a second. Jose looked ready to belt the woman. I grabbed Scott's arm to yank him out of the car, but there wasn't much need. He'd seized the moment and was halfway out the door.

"Drop it!" one of the women ordered.

A large gun appeared in her hands. I dove for the ground. Scott was right next to me as we tried scrambling away.

I glanced back and saw Jose try to raise his weapon out of his purse. One of the woman knocked it away. The glass of the car window shattered as bullets crashed through it.

The women dropped to the ground firing as they dodged. Jose jumped into the car. Seconds later, they roared away. Tires screeched as one car a half block down and one on the cross street gave chase.

I got up and dusted myself off.

"Thank you. Who are you?" I asked.

"Police," the woman in the black skirt said.

The other pulled a radio out of her purse and spoke into it. She gave the license number and a description of the car to whoever was on the other end of the line. "Shots fired. Need some assistance here."

"You guys okay?" the one who spoke first asked.

"Yeah," I said. "You saved our lives."

She shrugged. Several blue-and-white cop cars pulled up. People jumped out and slammed doors. Various cops began filling out forms, making sketches, and asking questions. Some concern was expressed about where the bullets had gone that Equelle had fired. They found two lodged in a Dumpster in the alley next to us and one in the brick wall right next to it. Fortunately they hadn't gone into any of the surrounding high rises.

The women told us that our building had been under surveillance. Jose and I had been spotted entering. They didn't know who she was, but as soon as I was spotted, pairs of cops had begun to converge on the building from three different directions. They didn't close in right away because they weren't sure what was happening or where Scott was.

Before telling the rest of our story, we told the cops about Angelo and Bernie in the hotel. Calls were made, and a couple of cops hopped in one car and streaked off. Eventually we got permission to enter the penthouse, although a platoon of cops came with us. I didn't care. I felt secure with a horde of them in the living room.

I took a shower and shaved in a still-unreconstructed bathroom. Scott did the same. I let the warm water cascade over me and felt the heat sink into my tense muscles. Near the end, I began to shake from the memory of what had almost happened to us.

Wrapped in a towel I entered the bedroom. I was drawn to the picture of Scott and me that always sat on the end table on my side of the bed. He always slept on the right nearest the door to the rest of the apartment. I always slept nearest the window. It was just the opposite when we spent nights at my place. I picked up the photo and gazed at it. It was a shot taken in St. Louis of the two of us smiling and laughing in front of an elephant we had just ridden on. The elephant had its trunk draped over one of Scott's shoulders, and my hand hung over his other. It was a goofy picture, but it was one of my favorites because it showed Scott and me enjoying life and each other. He looked beautiful and strong and sexy. I got misty eyed.

I heard Scott enter the room. He padded up behind me.

I got tears in my eyes and pulled him close. "I never want to lose you," I said.

"I love you so much," he said.

With cops scattered around our living room, we didn't have time to linger. We dressed in faded blue jeans, white socks, running shoes, and sweatshirts. His from the University of Arizona, mine from UCLA.

I had time to check the answering machine for messages. One was from Bill Proctor, saying he had to meet us; the other was from Lester, asking how things were going. I managed to get Proctor at his dad's estate. He wouldn't tell me what he wanted on the phone. I got the impression that he thought the phones might be tapped or someone might be listening. As paranoid as his dad was, maybe his security included in-house surveillance. I was tired and didn't want to meet, but he sounded desperate as he insisted. I didn't know how long we'd be tied up with the cops. He didn't want to come to the penthouse. We wrangled for a few minutes, but I finally agreed to call him when we finished with the cops. He told me he was leaving home then and gave me his car-phone number. I told him to be careful and that if for some reason he needed to get hold of me, he could call the answering machine and leave a message.

The greeting on Lester's answering machine consisted of the first four notes of Beethoven's Fifth Symphony. I told the tape I'd call back.

Back in the living room we found that Bolewski and Quinn had joined the crowd of cops.

Scott and I sat together on the couch.

Quinn said, "We need you to tell us exactly what happened."

We told them the story. Before we started, the other cops had been dismissed, except two who were told to stay at the front door.

"Why aren't you convinced we need protection? That

something strange and horrible is going on?" I looked from one to the other.

"We've got a few questions," Quinn said. "Nobody saw the body except you. We found no evidence of anything strange in the tunnels. Would they clean that well?"

"It happened," I said.

"You say Proctor was here and that he came from Mexico," Quinn continued. "And you say that according to this Brad Stawalski and the necklace guys, Glen had the addresses of a safe house for drug kingpins here in Chicago and maybe other cities?"

I nodded.

Bolewski stated the obvious. "We've got to talk to all three of these guys."

"He claimed he was only a guard for Glen. I can't picture Glen Proctor relying on Brad. Glen had to be using him in some way."

"I hope we find him alive to ask him," Quinn said. "Until then we have to concentrate on what Glen was doing. We have a record of him entering Mexico in late September. From twelve days ago, no one has any idea of where he's been. We have had people hunting through computers working on airline records for any international flight coming into O'Hare. We can find no record of Glen Proctor entering the country on any flight from anywhere, and that took a lot of hours of checking all the airlines."

"Maybe he flew to another city, or maybe he didn't fly," I said. "At least under his own name."

"Could he have entered the country some other way?" Scott asked. "Walked across the border?"

"We're not sure about that," Quinn said, "and we have no way of checking every city in the country." He took a deep breath. "What did turn up in the records is that Scott Carpenter flew into Chicago on Air Mexico on Friday. He left from Acapulco, had a two-hour stopover in Dallas to change planes, and then flew here."

"I've been here or at our cabin in Wisconsin since the end of the season," Scott said.

"You'll have to prove that," Bolewski said.

"I've got all kinds of witnesses," Scott said. "I've been in the city, and people up around the cabin know me. It'll be real easy to establish that I was here."

I said, "He's not the only guy named Scott Carpenter on the planet, or Proctor could have been using his name."

"We've interviewed the stewardesses on the flight," Quinn said. "They said this was a baseball player bragging about his accomplishments, demanding special attention, and trying to get dates with three of them."

"That proves it wasn't me," Scott said. "I wouldn't be trying to get a date with anybody, and if I was, it would be with a steward."

"Could have been a cover," Bolewski said.

"Did it look like me?" Scott asked.

"They remembered blond and muscular and blue-eyed," Quinn said.

"I'm not built anything like Proctor," Scott said. "He was shorter by three inches. He was built more compact and beefier."

"Fortunately, neither of you has committed a crime that we're sure of yet," Bolewski said. "We're just trying to track down your story."

"Have you found out anything more about the shots that were fired Saturday morning?" I asked.

"Absolutely nothing. No trace of the guys. No useful descriptions of them. The car they abandoned in the intersection after chasing you was stolen in Des Moines a week ago."

"Wait a second," Scott said. "You can't just forget about Proctor using my name. Maybe that's why they're after us."

"Wouldn't he have to have a passport made out in

Scott's name?" I asked. "Can he do that? How could he do that?"

"Possible," Quinn said. "If he had a fake passport, then this isn't some spur-of-the-moment thing that he was involved in."

I said, "He's been doing illegal things for years, and this was probably only one of his covers."

Scott looked miserable.

We went round and round on the Glen Proctor murder, the chase through the tunnels, the shots outside of our building, and all the possible illegal things Glen may have been into. The cops hadn't picked up Equelle, Jose, or Brad yet. This lapse did not boost my confidence in the Chicago Police Department. We spent a huge amount of time on the folderol that you must have something or know something that you don't know you have or think you have, and what could it be? We had no idea.

Ultimately it boiled down to the question I asked: "What the hell are we supposed to do now?"

We obviously weren't safe. We certainly needed to come to some kind of terms with those after us, but we had no idea what those terms were or whether they could even be met. Glen Proctor had involved us deeply in his illegal schemes, and I couldn't see any way out. My irritation with Scott for getting us into this seeped back into my consciousness.

"You need to understand," Quinn said. "Your story sounds strange, but we've found some stuff that bears out the theory that you're in danger, but we don't see any solution soon. The little scene outside this place gives a lot of credence to your story, but we eliminate no possibility until this is completely cleared up."

This set off another drop in my confidence in the cops' competence. "We need some assurance of our own safety," I said.

"Maybe you should try and hire more guards," Quinn suggested.

"That really worked last time," I said.

"Also, the Mexican authorities want to talk to you," Bolewski said.

Scott exploded. He jumped to his feet and flung his arms out. "We! Don't! Know! Anything!" He paced to the left a few steps then to the right, coming back to stand in front of the cops. "We are innocent! We haven't done anything!"

"They aren't going to accuse you or try to extradite you," Quinn said. "They just want information."

"We've told you everything! If we knew any more, don't you think we'd have given it to you already?" Scott asked. He walked to the window and pounded his fist against it hard enough to make it shake. We watched him in silence.

"This is total bullshit!" he said to the expanse of buildings and sky outside.

The intercom phone rang from downstairs. It was a cop asking for Quinn.

"Be careful," Scott said.

Quinn frowned at him. He listened to the receiver for a minute, hung it up and looked at us. "It's your lawyer."

A minute later Todd Bristol, in his usual go-to-court lawyer's drag, swept into the apartment.

"It's on the radio," he said. "That you were attacked. That the guards were captured. There is an army of reporters downstairs. *What* is going on?"

We told him.

When we finished, he said, "This is not credible."

I said, "Believe it. We were there."

"We're supposed to go meet the Mexican authorities," Scott said.

"I'll go with you," Todd said. "It actually might be good to go talk to them. They might have some insight into who and what is going on."

"Can we do this now—today—and get it over with?" I asked.

Todd consulted with the cops, and phone calls were made. Minutes later, we had an appointment to see a delegation at the Mexican consulate in the Prudential Building in a couple hours. Bolewski and Quinn said they'd talked twice today with the same Mexican authorities. We would go without them.

After they questioned Todd thoroughly about the guards, the firm they worked for, and Todd's connection with them, the cops got ready to leave.

"We're leaving with you," I said.

"I've arranged for more security guards," Todd said.

"That didn't work last time, although I think we should try it again," I said. To the police I said, "If you could come down to the parking garage with us, we'll get my truck. You can at least see us out of here safely." I realized that Lester's car was still parked near the Hotel Chicago. Todd said he'd take care of it later. I gave him the keys.

"Can we drive directly to the security people?" Scott asked.

"Let me make a call," Todd said.

"I don't want just two guys again," I said. "We need an army."

The cops agreed to wait while Todd called. He came back and said, "It's all set. We can meet them at the office."

"Why not wait for them here?" Scott asked.

"We're vulnerable here if the cops leave," I said. We took the elevator to the garage.

I had the driver's side door open before Scott said, "Shouldn't we have it checked for bombs?"

I dropped my hand from the door and left it open.

"How paranoid are we supposed to be?" I asked.

"We can't hang around here forever," Quinn said.

"Call the bomb squad," Todd ordered.

Bolewski didn't look happy at the sound of his command, but Quinn shrugged his shoulders. He used his radio to call in the request. Bolewski and Quinn agreed to wait until they arrived.

The cops stood off to the side. Todd regaled us with thoughts on how to handle the press, who was after us, and what we could do. His suggestions on the last were not the most helpful. He just kept saying, "Don't trust anyone. Don't leave the protection of the guards."

Bolewski and Quinn left when the bomb squad showed.

You could see your face in the gleaming black side of my truck. With its oversized tires, it towered over much of the rest of traffic. It was probably the butchest thing I ever bought, not counting the complete leather outfit I gave Scott as a gift last Christmas. Watch the most beautiful blond star pitcher in baseball put that on for the first time and turn to you and gaze at you from under the brim of his leather cap, and you've got one turned-on hot puppy.

The back of the pickup had served as one of our hottest ever lovemaking sessions when we pulled off the road on a trip through North Dakota. We were near Sykeston on an unlit dirt road, under a full moon, the entire Milky Way as our only witness. We lay in the back on top of our tents, sleeping bags, and mounds of camping gear. We made mad passionate love. It was the first and only camping trip we ever took. This sleeping on the ground or on cots can be mildly romantic, but I'd done my stint as a kid and in the marines. Scott was cured of his desire to inflict us on nature when he found a live rattlesnake that had crawled into his sleeping bag to cool off. That particular dash to the hospital had been the immediate cause for our giving all our gear to a gay thrift shop.

I thought the set of tools stored between the seat and rear of the truck's cab added a nice macho touch. Scott knew how to use all of them. I barely recognized one or two.

A few minutes later the bomb squad reported all clear on my truck and Scott's Porsche.

Todd, Scott, and I clambered into the cab of the truck.

I zigged and zagged through the early Monday evening traffic of Streeterville. As far as I could tell, nobody followed us.

8

"I'm hungry," Scott said.

We were heading west on Ontario Street. Without a word, I swung into the Rock-and-Roll McDonald's, claimed to be the busiest one in the world. There were only two cars in front of us in line. I pulled to the drive up and looked at my passengers. Todd sniffed. I thought that if we were back in the Victorian era at this moment, he'd have put his handkerchief to his mouth and had a spell. Scott and I ordered a lean burger each and some diet soda. Scott also got a vanilla milk shake. I controlled myself from such excess. I knew he probably wouldn't finish it all, and I'd get a lot of it. We ate as I drove, Todd and the dashboard holding the excess provender. I wound up draining the last third of the shake. I knew it would probably make me head for the john fairly soon, but I couldn't resist the vanilla treat.

As we drove down Orleans Street, Todd asked the question. "How did you guys get into this anyway?"

I blurted it out before I could stop myself. "Scott didn't listen to me. Proctor took advantage of him. I warned him."

"You aren't my parents," Scott said. "I wanted to be kind to somebody. That's not a bad thing."

"He wouldn't have been able to turn to us if you'd listened to what I said the first time you brought him home."

This hadn't been the first time Glen Proctor stayed at our place.

"So you're psychic. You know the future. You always knew this was going to happen?"

"I know you shouldn't have had anything to do with him. Your judgment wasn't so good in this case."

"Like there have been other cases?"

"I'm not saying that."

"Then what are you saying? That it's my fault that we're in this? I feel like shit about everything that's happened to us, but you don't have to rub it in. That's what you always try to do, rub it in."

"I was just pointing out—"

"That's what you always try to do; just point out, and what you mean is that I've screwed up again. I don't want to be just pointed out anymore. I don't need . . ."

"You're not being fair . . ."

"You didn't let me finish . . ."

"If you'd just listen . . ."

Since we were shouting at the same time, we couldn't hear what the other was saying anyway. At the corner of Orleans and Chicago, I almost bashed the truck into the back of a bus. The screeching tires and motion that flung us forward silenced our argument. Wrappers and cartons got flung around the cab.

Todd spoke into the silence. "I'm sorry. I shouldn't have brought it up. I've been friends with you both a long time. Why don't we let it rest until the danger is past?"

I wanted to tell him to shut up, but then I'd feel even more like a petulant schoolboy. I felt awful for yelling at Scott, but I was too angry to take it back. The fury and the frustration of the past few days had just boiled over.

We both grumbled agreement to Todd's suggestion. We proceeded in silence.

I was also embarrassed about fighting in front of someone. I used to always be angry at my parents for their insistence that you keep your mouth shut in front of guests. They could have been arguing furiously a minute before guests began to arrive for a party; but when people showed up, they were perfect host and hostess. I always thought it was blatant hypocrisy until I got older and far too many of my coupled friends used the occasion of someone's visit to needle, nag, or tear into their mates. Now I felt awful for fighting in front of Todd.

I took Chicago Avenue over to Halsted and up to Goose Island. The security firm had headquarters in one of the plethora of converted warehouses that teemed in this neighborhood. I parked the car on Bliss Street in a no-parking zone exactly in front of the entrance. I didn't want to be on the street for one second longer than necessary. At least the lack of traffic in the area was a minor assurance that we hadn't been followed.

The front desk had one clerk monitoring a switchboard alive with blinking lights. We waited patiently for a break. When we finally had his attention, Todd told him he needed to speak to Anton Frobisher.

"Mr. Frobisher is in a meeting and can't be disturbed," the functionary said.

"Tell him it's Todd Bristol," Todd commanded. He used a lawyerly voice that got through to the clerk.

The connection was made, words were spoken, and a minute later we were ushered into a room with nine people in it. A few sat at a large conference table. One talked on a phone in a corner. Most stood in clumps talking earnestly. They wore the kind of clothes you wear on a quiet evening at home. A few wore security-guard uniforms.

One man separated himself from the group and came over. Introductions over Frobisher said, "We're here because of the failure of Bernie and Angelo. Nothing like that has ever happened to the firm. They are good men. Mostly we've got contracts with businesses, banks, factories, like that. A few years ago, one of our bank guards was wounded. That's the worst that's ever happened. That you got kidnapped is awful. Everybody is really upset."

Todd told them we needed more guards. I thought this would be a simple request, but Anton brought this news to a group to our right, and soon the entire assemblage faced us in a semicircle. Debate raged among them over whether or not they should supply more guards to us. The crux of the problem was the obvious and immediate danger.

"You can't refuse us," Todd said at one point. "These men need protection, and that's what you do."

This brought outrage and anger from some of them. Finally Anton said, "Todd, you've been a friend for a long time, and we'd like to help; but even if we said yes, I'm not sure any of our operatives would agree to the job."

"They're your employees," Todd said. "They have to do what you say."

"Within reason," Anton said.

"Isn't danger supposed to be an assumed part of their job?" Todd asked. "After all, they do carry guns. They're supposed to protect people."

Anton admitted this was so.

"Maybe if you told them they'd be guarding Scott Carpenter, the baseball player," Todd said. "That should convince some of them."

Fortunately, no fuss had been made about Scott's fame so far. These people were too upset by events to go into a fan mode.

Anton said, "We can try, but we won't force anyone to take on this job. It would be bad for the company. What if you guys decided to sue?"

"We don't want to file a lawsuit," I said. "We just want protection."

"Is there another company?" Scott asked.

"Not that I've dealt with," Todd said.

Within an hour, three guards showed up, pulled in perhaps by the lure of Scott's name or the hint of danger, or simply because they needed the overtime.

We formed a caravan of three vehicles. Two men, Frank and Jack, rode in an Oldsmobile in front of us, and Bruno, who looked like a former linebacker, rode in his fifteen-year-old Chevy pickup behind us.

We took Chicago Avenue all the way east to Michigan Avenue and then south to the Prudential Building, where the Mexican consulate was housed. On the way, Todd informed us that many countries located their consulates in various business skyscrapers, concentrated on the east side of the Loop. Scott and I did not exchange a word.

The parking garage was quiet. We were the only ones on the elevator. We were forced to stop on the first floor and sign in and, after a call to the consular offices, we resumed our ride up the elevator.

On the twentieth floor, we emerged into a foyer with gray carpeting and white walls. To the right were the offices of a law firm. To the left was a hall, down which we saw the lights coming from only one room.

The offices consisted of a large reception area, a conference room, and three private offices. Travel posters promoting the joys of vacationing in Mexico filled the walls.

Four people met us. A man and a woman, both in their early forties, were introduced as Mexican police officers. Another woman was from the Mexican Fine Arts Museum. The fourth was a man from the consular office.

Before the meeting started, I called Bill Proctor's car phone and told him we now had guards and could meet him at our place.

We sat in the conference room, which had a view of Grant Park, the Art Institute a block or two away, and the traffic on Michigan Avenue. Our guards sat in the outer office.

Introductions over, I explained what had been happening to us. I finished with: "We understand the Frederico

Torres connection from all that's been told to us. Can you help us out of this mess?"

The woman cop, who seemed to be the spokesperson for the group, said, "We'll help all we can, but unfortunately it may not be much. We are also very much in the dark. We have three possible problems: drugs, jewels, and relics."

Her name was Rosarita Montez. She wore a gray skirt, white blouse, and a thin gold chain around her neck. Her lustrous black hair was pulled back in a ponytail. She continued. "Because of Glen Proctor, your lives are now entwined with the drug cartels. You had a firsthand experience with how dangerous that is. What you don't know is that we became suspicious of Glen Proctor some time ago."

"He was a problem before?" I asked.

"His father and mother have many business dealings in Mexico that are honorable and are a great help to our country," said the consular official.

Rosarita didn't ignore him or seem angry, but she dug in her heels. "We came here with the knowledge that Glen appeared in the presence of both Pedro and Frederico Torres, who are now archrivals. We are reasonably certain Glen was using the name Scott Carpenter."

"So he'd planned this for some time," I said. "If he had a fake passport and everything."

"We don't have all those proofs," Rosarita said. "What we do know is that he hung around each of them for several days. Your information tells us what he found. We have no evidence that his father or mother had or have dealings with the drug lords."

"But you have suspicions," Scott said.

"We check out every possible lead," she said.

I wished we could talk to her without the consular official present. Maybe it would be possible later.

"Pedro and his brother broke about two years ago.

Pedro is the head of a paramilitary group consisting mostly of people who have grievances against Frederico, probably over the spoils of the drug trade."

The male cop, Hidalgo Lopez, said, "The rivalry is bitter. Anyone getting mixed up in their fight could be killed by either side. We don't know what kind of deal he was trying to make."

"There are huge rewards on both Pedro's and Frederico's heads," Rosarita said.

"How much is huge?" I asked.

"Over seven million on Frederico, around a million on Pedro. The international community wants these guys."

"Glen would be tempted by either reward," I said.

The cops glanced at each other.

"Glen had lots of plans and schemes," I said. "Each was more ludicrous than the next. He could have got himself into anything to make some money." Remembering the talk with his brother Bill, I said, "Glen desperately wanted to prove himself to his father and mother by making a success of himself. He knew his baseball career was dead. He wanted to try and make a quick killing in Mexico and come back and show them how well he could do."

"So," Todd said, "he could have been dealing drugs or dealing in drug lords. My clients know nothing of all this."

"But they must think you do," Rosarita said. "By using the name of Scott Carpenter, he involved you deeply."

"We know," I said.

"They came to my place to kill me," Scott said. "Whoever it was thought it was me because he used my name. We looked enough alike so that someone could easily have mistaken us."

"I don't mean to sound ignorant," Hildalgo said, "but to many of my people all North Americans look alike."

"So if he found something out, where is the proof?" I asked. "Where is the threat to these people? What did Glen do with it? We don't have it. In this case, they killed the right person—by accident." How close Scott came to being murdered because of Glen's stupid schemes I didn't like to think. "They are still after us; therefore something remains a threat. Stawalski said Glen was sending his information north, not taking it with him. Where is it? They must not have it."

"The assumption must be that you were working together with him. Where did he go the first night he came back to this country? To your place. Somehow they think you know."

"And there's no way to meet with them?" Scott said. "To try to reason?"

"Children, babies, whole families have died in the drug wars. They wouldn't care about killing someone they didn't know and was even a remote danger. Information such as Brad Stawalski described would be plenty threatening enough for them to still be after you."

"Why not just change everything?" I asked. "Why keep bothering us?"

"Maybe it is easier to get rid of you than to upset their plans. You want to move from comfortable safe houses because some rich punk idiot finds information? Maybe Proctor stumbled onto their main distribution route and plans into this country. He might not have told Stawalski everything."

We talked about what to do for a while, but got nowhere. We just didn't know anything, and no one had any suggestions about what we could do to remove the threat. A drug summit between us and them to convince them we were innocent bystanders didn't seem likely to happen.

After thirty minutes of this, the consular official said, "There are other possibilities. Ms. Montez mentioned relics earlier. We should explain."

The archaeologists spoke up, "The traffic in pre-Columbian relics out of Mexico is a scandal. Illegal trafficking is outlawed, but it goes on. And then you have dealing in fake relics. We're talking about millions of dollars."

"Fake relics?" Scott asked.

"Oh, yes. People desperately want pre-Columbian artifacts. It has become much more difficult to get the real ones out of the country, although certainly not impossible. But enterprising thieves have managed to start a lucrative market in the fake items. Some of it is really poor quality, but that doesn't seem to matter. Selling fake art is hardly a phenomenon unique to Mexico."

"Let me get this straight," I said. "Glen could have been being chased by someone who had stolen a relic or a fake one?"

"Some are priceless. Unscrupulous collectors would pay a fortune for some of the finds. They pay huge sums of money for items that have little intrinsic value."

Hidalgo said, "Customs officials, police on both sides of the border, governments, try to stop the pillage. Brad Stawalski didn't tell you the whole story by half. Brad has been stumbling around the countryside trying to make a quick score. He's been to the diggings. He's been spotted with known relic thieves. Then he hooked up with Glen."

So Brad had been far from honest with us.

I'd sat for an hour of this when finally the vanilla shake from earlier began to rumble in my stomach. I squirmed in extreme discomfort for fifteen minutes. Finally I announced I had to use the john. I was given a key for a room down the hall.

As I exited the office area, Rosarita caught up to me. I didn't want to stop, but she grabbed my arm, "There is the real possibility that either Mr. or Mrs. Proctor, both of whom have great sums of money invested in Mexico, were behind some kind of deal that went bad. A diplomat would never make such a charge because the investment money from two such prominent real-estate people means a great deal to our country."

I told her we would have to talk more in a minute. I practically tore out of her arm. I hurried past the banks of elevators and darkened offices. At the far end of the corridor, I unlocked the john door and hurried in. Minutes later, feeling much relieved, I washed my hands. As I pulled down the towel to dry them, I thought I heard voices in the hall. Maybe others were taking an opportunity for a break.

I swung open the door, stepped into the hall, and instantly pulled myself back. I'd seen the back of a bald head. I knew he'd have a blond mustache that reached down below his chin.

I didn't hear feet running toward me, so I presumed I hadn't been spotted. I needed to go for help. The swiftness with which some of these groups killed might mean that Scott and the rest had only minutes or seconds to live.

Carefully I opened the door. I managed only a glimpse of three men with machine guns watching the corridor outside the office I'd been in. I was too far away to make a rush toward them down the hall. I had no weapon, so I needed a plan. I had to get out.

But all possibility of plans soon vanished. I heard voices again. I heard loud protests for a few moments from one of the Mexican cops. I heard a slight thud, a gasp, and no more protests. I waited behind the shut john door. I checked the ceiling to see if it was the kind you could remove the tiles from and crawl away through the ceiling. It wasn't.

If I was caught here, there was no escape. I listened intently. I heard the elevator doors open and, a minute later, close. No sounds penetrated through the washroom door.

I checked my watch. I waited a minute, then two. Finally I eased the washroom door open.

The first thing I saw was the remnants of the top of the head of Hidalgo, the Mexican cop. The pop and thud I'd heard had been his taking a bullet between his eyes. A large portion of his brains was smeared on the wall and carpet behind and under his head.

Still I heard no sound.

I continued inching the door open. The corridor was empty. I eased myself into the hall, still listening. I crept down the carpet past the still-warm body and toward the conference room we'd been in.

One of the guards lay crumpled on the ground. His head was in worse shape than the Mexican cop's. The only thing moving besides me in the office were drops of blood from the corpses.

I grabbed the nearest phone and dialed 911. The dispatcher told me to stay put. The cops would be here in seconds.

I hurried to the elevator. I wasn't about to wait while they could be hurting Scott. I pressed the down and up buttons. It might have been all of twenty seconds before the elevator arrived. I thought it might have been hours.

As the doors opened, I flattened myself against the wall. No gun barrel peeked out. No person emerged. I leaped on and pushed the button for the ground floor. The car made no stops on the way down. In the lobby, the security people looked at me in bewilderment. Obviously, captors and captured hadn't gone this way. I ran to the parking-garage level. The attendant in the booth at the exit gate was outside and cursing while clutching shards of the broken gate in his hands.

I rushed to my truck, jammed the key in the ignition, shoved it into gear, and roared toward the exit. The parking attendant held up his hands to try and stop me. I gunned the engine. He leaped out of the way.

I pulled to the edge of the driveway on Randolph Street and stopped. They must have gone right because Randolph is one way going west, but no vehicle was stopped at the light at the corner of Michigan Avenue. Traffic farther down Randolph toward the west and on Michigan going north and south flowed normally. I'd been in a big rush and had absolutely nowhere to go. No vehicle description. No idea where they might have taken Scott, what they might have done with the other people. I could wait for the cops, or I could search.

The parking attendant hurried up. I interrupted his imprecations early on. "What kind of car just drove out?" I asked.

He continued to berate me. I opened the door, climbed down, and grabbed the guy by the front of his shirt. I didn't have time to remember Miss Manners's Guide to Throttling Important Information Out of Someone. By the time I got through to him and found out they had left in a black van, there wasn't one anywhere in sight. I sat back in my truck, put my hands at the twelve o'clock position on the steering wheel, and rested my head on them. I could race around and around endless blocks in ever-widening concentric circles and drive for hours uselessly, or I could sit there in frustration and fear. I wanted to choose neither, but my choice was made for me by the arrival of building security, with the cops mere seconds behind them. And then it was an hour of questioning.

Of course, Bolewski and Quinn showed up. I don't remember giving anyone a reasonable or even sensible answer. All I knew was that Scott was gone and in danger, and I was helpless.

I called Bill Proctor's car phone again and told him the latest. He was aghast and asked whether he could help. He insisted that it was more important than ever that we meet. I needed to think. Reluctantly I agreed to meet him at nearby Buckingham Fountain in half an hour.

When the cops were finished talking to me, Quinn was nice enough to offer to have somebody drive me home, or to call somebody to get me.

I told him no.

He said, "We've still got cops outside your building, and one of ours is doing security. You'll be able to go home tonight."

"After I find Scott," I said.

It was midnight, time to meet Bill Proctor. I wondered why he'd been so insistent about having to meet. Maybe he'd have information that would lead to Scott. I returned to my truck and made a slow exit down Randolph Street, then south on Michigan. I took Monroe Street, with the Art Institute and the Petrillo Music Shell on my right, then continued out to Lake Shore Drive. I wanted to make a complete circuit of Grant Park and the area around the fountain before I made any stops. I wanted to check for possible traps and to see whether I was being followed.

Grant Park was constructed from the dregs of the great Chicago Fire of 1871. The good citizens took the debris from the conflagration and dumped it in the lake to create a park. Buckingham Fountain, which sat in the middle, had long since been turned off for the winter.

I made a complete circuit of the rectangle around the fountain: out Monroe to Lake Shore Drive, south to Balbo Drive, and west back to Columbus Drive. I craned my neck in all directions at every second, paying just enough attention to traffic to avoid an accident. As it was I got honked at viciously and heard brakes squealing behind me when I pulled back onto Columbus going north.

During the day, it was almost impossible to park on Columbus Drive; but at this time on a Monday night, especially with the dank and dreary weather, fewer than half the parking spaces were filled.

I pulled up to the light, where Congress Parkway runs into Grant Park. I was three cars from the intersection with two cars behind and a line of traffic on my left. With the oversized wheels, the view from my truck gave me an excellent perspective over the tops of all the vehicles. Finally I spotted Bill Proctor standing next to the fountain. I took another look around. The line of cars in the lane on my left inched forward enough so that a red Toyota pulled up next to me. The passenger-side window slid down a few inches, and I saw the glint of the barrel of a gun.

No car was parked on my right. I swung the truck over and jumped the curb. As the wheels thumped and rumbled, I heard several shots and the glass in the back of the cab shattered. Another bullet struck the roof. I raced over the pavement to Proctor, threw open the door, and shouted, "Get in!"

He looked bewildered. The thought flashed through my head that maybe he was part of an elaborate setup. Or whoever was shooting was after him, too. He tumbled into the cab. Before he had the door shut, I tromped my foot onto the gas pedal. Too many trees stood in the way to drive over the grassy portions of the park. I rushed to the top of the stairs that led down to Lake Shore Drive, slammed on the brakes, eased up on the pedal, then thudded down the stairs. I glanced in the rearview mirror. They weren't following through the park, but it would take them only a minute or two to hurry around the park and come back this way. The traffic southbound was light. I swung the car to the right and sped toward the Field Museum of Natural History.

"What the hell is going on?" Proctor asked.

"Your fucking brother has managed to screw up a whole lot of everything! Bodies are piling up at an alarming rate. I might ask you the same questions. What the hell is going on? Why are we meeting here and now? Who are all these people?"

"I don't know," Proctor said. "Honest to God, I don't know what's going on, but I'm here because I want to help. I couldn't get away from the house any earlier. I think I found out some things."

I roared past the museum and swung to the right to get into the lanes for the Stevenson Expressway. I wanted to get as far away as possible from any pursuit as quickly as I could. One thought blared in my head. Save Scott. Find him. Rescue him. Absolutely no one and nothing was going to get in my way for that. I thought of our fight in the car. Those weren't going to be the last words I ever said to him. When I saw him again, I'd never stop saying "I love you."

Proctor was silent for several minutes as we drove southwest down the Stevenson. He wore faded blue jeans that clung to his slender waist and hips with no belt. His shoes and socks were white. He wore an Oxford University sweatshirt.

The radio was playing jangling jazz on WNIB. I flicked it off. Noise was not what I needed. Out past Damen Avenue, I drummed my fingers on the wheel, clutched at it with white-knuckled fists, tapped my foot against the floor, or rapped my knuckles against the window.

At around Cicero Avenue, Proctor said, "Tell me what's happened."

"Your brother is responsible for the danger my lover is in at this moment."

My tone didn't invite conversation. He kept quiet until we passed First Avenue.

"Do you want to know what I found out?" he asked.

At La Grange Road, I said, "Yes."

"I've always been neutral during my parents' fights as best I could. For a kid, that's tough. They always want to get me on one or the other's side. I've got contacts in both organizations that I can go to for information."

"Why didn't you just ask your mom or dad what's going on? Wouldn't whichever one knows the truth want to tell so they could get you on their side?"

"Maybe neither one knows the truth. Or wants to tell me the truth," he said.

I pulled onto the ramp from the outbound Stevenson to the northbound Tri-State Tollway. I cruised through the eternally-under-reconstruction road.

"In the past couple of years, but especially with the new North American Free Trade Agreement, there's been a lot more activity on setting up more business in Mexico. Like jockeying for position trying to open more *maquiladoras.*"

"What's that?" I asked.

"Them. *Maquiladoras* are factories in Mexico where they assemble imported parts for reexport to this country without tariffs. They pay Mexican workers far below the minimum wage in the United States to manufacture products way cheaper than they can in America."

"I understand."

"Anyway, my sources said Glen was supposed to be helping with some of the dealing and getting information for my mother on my dad's projects, but he was working for him at the same time."

I told him I knew this.

"Well, what happened is that they found that out down there in Mexico, too. So my dad's security people and my mom's security people were after him. To find him and to figure out what he was doing. He was in big trouble. My mom and dad were supposed to go down there. They were supposed to have some big confrontation between them with Glen as the sort of go-between, or hostage, or sacrificial lamb, depending on who got to him first."

"So what happened?"

"The big meeting never came off. Everybody flew down to Mexico, but Glen disappeared. My source says he thought Glen hooked up with some of his old drug buddies. Both of my parents had people searching for Glen, and they began to run across drug groups and relic groups hunting for him."

"A couple of people and the Mexican authorities told us about some of the drug and relic business." I explained what had happened at the Prudential Building.

"Damn!" he said. "They could all die," he said very softly.

"I've got to find Scott," I said.

"There's supposed to be a big meeting here between my mom and dad and their security people. Something strange is going on."

"Somebody else knows for sure he's dead. Your mom seemed genuinely surprised when we told her."

Glen's eyes misted over. "Could one of them have killed him?" he asked.

"I don't know." I hoped not, for Bill Proctor's sake.

"I'd like to be there for the big meeting," I said.

"I don't know where or when it is," Bill said.

"Would your sources tell you?"

"Maybe. I can at least ask."

"I wish we could find that stuff he was supposed to send north."

"I don't know how," Glen said.

I thought about it until we neared the Deerfield Toll Plaza. I had to go north to the next exit, turn around, enter the tollway going south, and take the extension toward the Edens Expressway.

"At your house you mentioned that Glen sent a drug shipment up here for his high-school buddies. How did he do that?"

"The best way to send drugs to this country is to ship them in with regular stuff that would normally be coming north. You just add it to the regular shipping invoice as whatever it's supposed to be. Tea sets, spoons, light bulbs, whatever. You mislabel the stuff. It gets past customs and comes up here. This smuggling-it-over-the-border shit is small time. The really big stuff comes in legitimately. There's too much for it to be smuggled piecemeal."

"You sound like you know all about it," I said.

"I have nothing to do with drugs or smuggling," Bill said flatly. "You can believe that or not. I'm helping you because something happened to my brother. I want to know why he died and who is responsible. I loved him. I'm going to get to the bottom of it. If we can help each other, great. If not, that's fine, too."

We drove in silence the entire length of the Edens to the junction with the Kennedy Expressway.

Bill said, "The information on the Torres people. Why did Glen want to send that north? So that he would have a copy to use as leverage to save his skin if he got caught?"

"If he thought that, it didn't work."

"Or if he made the threat to them, maybe they figured

they could get the information some other way and didn't need him."

I said, "Or he told them Scott and I had it, so they killed him and came after us? The bastard!"

"He might have been desperate. I don't know what I'd say in that situation. I'm not sure anybody would."

I wanted to avoid fighting with Bill about his brother. I'd had one awful argument, and while I wasn't close to Bill Proctor, I didn't need more grief and guilt.

"Sending the information would probably require copies. He wouldn't want to keep something like that with him. He'd have backups. So where would they be?"

"No packages of any kind came to our house today. I saw the mail first."

"Could have come to one of your parents."

"Maybe, but these guys were after *you.* There's got to be a connection with you guys."

"It could still be in the mail or in one of those delivery services."

"Didn't you tell me Glen promised to tell you guys everything on Sunday?"

"Yeah."

"Maybe that's what he was waiting for: the delivery."

"Post office is closed on Sundays and today, for that matter. It's Columbus Day. Glen did seem awful nervous when we left for the fund-raiser the other night. Maybe it was because his package hadn't come."

"So it had to be some company that delivers on weekends."

"Who does that?"

"I don't know."

I realized I was supposed to be in school within a few hours, teaching teenagers the mysteries of the writing process. If I didn't find Scott, I wouldn't be there.

I was near downtown Chicago, so I pulled off at the Ohio Street off ramp and drove to Scott's place. I walked up to the blue-and-white squad car outside and announced that

I was going in. I asked for an escort. The attractive dark-haired cop with a bushy mustache led us upstairs. He inspected the premises and declared them free of hostile people. He left.

Bill and I looked in the phone book and called every delivery company available. From the post office's 800 number, we got the number and address for the overnight-express expediter in Chicago. No one answered the phone. It was just after two. We had numbers we could call back when they opened in the morning. I suggested try going over to the overnight-express office. Someone had to be there to be doing the overnight-express sorting didn't they? It seemed like quite a useless endeavor, but we had no other leads, and I was desperately frightened for Scott.

"You never know about the post office," Bill said as we drove over. "They make all kinds of mistakes. If Glen sent it through them . . . who knows? A couple of times when I was in college my parents sent me stuff overnight express. It never got there the next day. They always got their money back."

The office was on the West Side—in fact, only four blocks from Mrs. Proctor's warehouse. We drove through the deserted streets. The only ones out were the homeless, who didn't mind the chilly but reasonably warm weather for October.

The office was the bottom floor of another formerly de-crepit warehouse. We found the doors in front locked, but around the back we found trucks being loaded and unloaded.

We were directed to an office in the center of the building. There we found a woman less than four feet high with two fingers on her left hand missing and a rash on her face that made her face look as if someone had dropped scalding water on it not five minutes ago. She smiled at us. Joanna Andrews was not only sympathetic, but incredibly helpful. She looked disappointed when we didn't have a receipt number from the packaging to give her, but she simply called up the computer and said, "We've got a million of these to go through. I can help you look. It's going to take a while to find something. How much time you got?"

"As much as it takes," I said.

We scrolled through record after record for over two hours. I was exhausted. We took a break for a cup of coffee.

"Are you supposed to be showing us all this?" Proctor asked.

"No," she said cheerfully, "but somebody who works for the post office has to be a nice person. I'm it, so don't get used to it."

Twenty minutes after we started working again, we found it. Joanna tapped the screen. "Package from Glen Proctor to Scott Carpenter. Supposed to be delivered to an address on Lake Shore Drive. Says here it arrived and was delivered on Saturday. Signed for by Beatrice. According to this, it's there."

"It's not," I said. "We don't have anybody named Beatrice working in the building. I'm sure of it."

Joanna scrolled a bit further. "Oh." She pressed another button. "Somebody dropped it back in a mailbox."

"Why?" I asked.

"Maybe Beatrice figured out it wasn't hers and was embarrassed to give it to anyone because they might say something like 'Look, stupid, how could you sign for something that is so obviously not yours?' "

"So where is it?" Bill asked.

"Here somewhere. They tried to deliver it today, but no one named Carpenter was home at the address given."

Minutes later she found it, and we were back in my truck ripping open the contents. The box was approximately two feet long, one foot wide, and one foot deep.

9

Bill Proctor ripped open the box. I turned on the dome light. He pulled out layers of wrapping paper.

"Aha!" he exclaimed.

I looked over. It was a five-inch-by-five-inch stone carving of an ugly head attached to a lumpy body.

"This is what people have been dying for?" I asked.

We found four more relics, all completely intact. No way did it look as if you could break them apart to reveal hidden jewels or wealth inside.

Carefully we unfolded each scrap of wrapping paper. Blank thin tissue and rough, coarse cardboard. Not a word written anywhere. I jumped down from the cab, hefted one of the relics, and prepared to dash it on the ground.

"Hold it!" Proctor commanded. He held the slightly shredded corner of the box. "There's paper with writing on it wedged in here!" He extricated it carefully.

It looked as if each flap of the box had been slit open and reglued. All of them contained information. The one I opened contained records of fake and real relics. Along with paper, Bill's had computer disks: one labeled Mom, the other Dad. On the paper were lists of names and dates and what looked to be notations in code.

Proctor held up the paper from the flap he'd been working on. He held it to the light. "These are addresses in cities around the world. There are only five. One is in Chicago."

My heart began to hammer. I snatched the paper from his hand. "This is what we're looking for. These must be the safe houses." I didn't recognize the address for the one in Chicago, but it had to be somewhere on the South Side.

"We've got to take all this to the police," Proctor said. "We've got to sort all this out."

I waved the paper with the addresses. "I'm going to take this and go get Scott. They must have taken him to this address."

Proctor didn't try to discourage me with "Maybe they took him someplace else. Can we be sure it's this place? Won't it be dangerous?" I wouldn't have listened anyway.

I floored the truck and sped away.

"I don't understand the computer stuff," Proctor said as we neared Lake Shore Drive.

"Got to be the work he was doing for your mom and dad down there."

"That stuff in code too, probably," he said.

I let Proctor out at the Chicago Hilton and Towers. He could grab a cab there and take everything to the police.

"You should wait for cops and backup on this," he said.

"No way. I'm not waiting for explanations, warrants, and plans. He's there. I'm going to get him."

He patted my shoulder. "I'll get this done quickly. Help is on the way."

Dawn was just breaking as I drove east to State Street and then back south to 26th Street. I paused. The lights of the city were still on. Most of the motorists still had their headlights on. My quarry was one more block south. I turned east once more to the middle of the block. The alley was dirt encrusted and garbage strewn, with broken buildings and ominous shadows; just what I wanted for cover in approaching the address I had. I eased into the alley, pulled the truck into low, and inched forward.

This alley was a delight of urban blight topped off with the elevated tracks. I rocked over potholes and dodged the metal pilings to the far end. I stopped and let the engine idle while I took in the scene. Three-quarters of the way down, at the other end of the block I faced, was an El station.

Three immense row houses were all that were left on the block between 27th and 28th streets with State Street on the west and Wabash on the east. The abandoned buildings on this block had been ripped down. What was left were three grand old dames of a bygone era before the Near North Side became a haven of the rich, when the Near South Side of Chicago was the place were the wealthy lived and played.

They clustered tightly together in a row on the west side of the street, facing toward the not-too-distant Williams Park.

The first house was a picturesque pile of red brick that abutted right onto the sidewalk. It may have been one of the first homes built here, and the street may have reached up to it. A cast-iron fence of poles, spaced six inches apart, began at the back of the building and extended twenty feet to the crumbling remnants of a cobblestoned alley. The fence turned and followed the property of all three houses and then turned back in at the far end.

No barriers divided the backyards. One lone tree sat just outside the property at the southeast side.

I pulled out and drove to the left down 26th Street. A few feet later, I made a right and turned onto Wabash. I cruised down the block, trying simultaneously to keep my eyes on the houses, watch where I was driving, and look inconspicuous. Half of the houses on my left were boarded up, and the other half looked as they wished they'd been.

I turned right on 27th Street and right again on State Street. I was moving directly in front of all three of the old mansions. None of the windows was broken out. Through a picture window on the first floor of the one on the corner,

I saw a lamp glowing. I continued on up State Street back to 25th and drove back to the alley and came back to resume my perch in the shadows. I parked as close as I could to the burnt-out hulk of the former home at the end of the alley.

The broken and crumbling back porch of the corner house across the street seemed to offer a possible egress. The fence started at the end of the porch, but the slats connecting porch to ground looked jagged and rotting in the dim streetlight. I had seen no other possibility of entering unobserved in my circuit around the houses. I waited for an old Plymouth to clank past me and struggle through the light at the corner. I let myself out of the cab and flitted from shadow to shadow in the gloom cast by the tracks. One last glance revealed that no lights shone on this side of the house. I rushed to the porch bottom, yanked two boards out of the way so I could fit, then plunged through the opening. On hands and knees, I scurried forward. The ground was packed dirt and debris. In the middle of the porch, streetlights and the new dawn shown enough for me to see an opening to a crawl space. Under the house, my hands immediately began to sink a good inch into the damp ground. The crawl space was so small that I was forced to use my knees and elbows to pull myself along.

I crawled through the mud and slime inch by inch. The first rat scuttled away on my right. It had to be a close relative of the huge rodents in the tunnels under the Loop. The second rat paused for a few seconds before running off to the left. The coming dawn and the streetlights barely illuminated more than a yard or two on either side of me, but it was enough to show me more rats. Their eyes were yellow- and red-rimmed, and they were now giving more hesitation before turning to run.

I had no light and no weapon, but I knew that somewhere in the labyrinth above me was Scott: captured, tortured, maybe dead. I tried burying that last thought, but knew with more certainty than the sunrise that if my lover

161

was dead, everyone responsible would die. The slime and ooze had long since soaked through the front of my sweat-shirt and pants. I rested my chin in the mud for a few seconds, lifting my eyes under my brows to see ahead.

One rat—perhaps bolder than the rest, or maybe crazed with rabies—took a step or two toward me. I knew I needed to keep moving. I plowed and elbowed through the muck. Rats now scampered a few feet, then stopped. I forced my knees and elbows and hands and torso, any-thing that could edge me forward, to move. I stopped every few feet for a quick examination of the floor inches from my head. I still hadn't found an opening into the houses. My assumption that there would be an opening—or that I would be able to see it—faded as I moved farther toward deeper darkness.

The occasional sound of the El pounding along nearby and a few stray cars were the only other sounds besides that of the creepy critters close to me.

My eyes grasped at any protuberance that might indi-cate an opening upward. Finally I caught sight of a cylindri-cal device off to my left. I inched through the muck, ignored the filth, and thought only of saving Scott. Minutes later, I arrived at what I guessed to be a hot-water heater. The crawl space here was wide enough that I could move on my hands and knees. I knew there had to be an access door nearby. I propped myself on one elbow and gently prodded on the ceiling of the crawl space. My elbow sank three inches into the slime. I made my way around the object, pausing to reach up and examine a space of about three square feet at a time above me. I hunted more by feel than by sight. My neck began to ache from the unnatural position in which I had to hold my head. I made a complete circuit, but found nothing. I needed to expand my area of feel. I lowered my arm from the last touch and looked back.

Patches of light leaked through in a few places. I could have waited until full morning, but the already-slim chances of finding Scott alive would have diminished even more. I also saw the movement of furry creatures. I wasn't planning on spending enough time down here to develop significant relationships with this branch of the vermin elite.

I peered into the darkness farther ahead. Was that another cylinder off to my right? Maybe. Did I stay around this one and search for the crawl-space entrance that had to be there, or try my luck with the next object? I decided to try the space in direct line between the two cylinders. I took two steps with each limb, looked and touched, and crawled on. On my fifth try, the ceiling gave slightly on my first push.

Now came the next problems. Would the opening be unlocked? If I pushed it open, would I find a roomful of bad guys staring at me amusedly with machine guns ready to blaze away, or would I have another chance of finding my lover?

Of course, I didn't have much choice. I flipped onto my back to get more leverage and pushed upward again. The ooze immediately sank into every part of my clothing that touched the ghastly goo under me.

The square of board gave a fraction more, and I saw lines of light appear around the edges. Was this good or bad? Did it mean that someone was in the room above with the light on, or was I seeing the glow from the first light of day shining through a window in the room? I was well under the middle of the three buildings. It hardly seemed that it could be an outside room. I pushed again. The door stuck. I swore. The squeak of verminous beasts sounded from about ten feet away from my head. I pushed again. Nothing.

I flipped onto my stomach. Yellow eyes edged away, but not far. I positioned my back against the only possible exit above me. I squatted down, resting the palms of my hands in the mire. I waited for the rumble of a passing El. It might have been five minutes—maybe at least ten—before I heard that glorious rumble. I tried to stand. The wood of the hatch ground into the bottom of my spine. I drove upward with all the strength of my legs, balancing myself on my fingertips.

Suddenly there was a horrendous squeal, that which a rusty hinge gives when being moved for the first time in years. I could tell that any critters nearby scattered, because their squeaks disappeared. I dropped to my knees and twisted around. The sound of the El faded. I hoped it had been enough to cover the noise. I listened carefully for any steps on the floor above. I hadn't heard any so far. I waited as long as I could bear in stillness. I wouldn't need to issue an invitation to attack to the denizens of the underworld above.

I pushed at the square of ceiling. I could move it maybe an inch and a half. I thought of pounding at it. I waited for another El to pass, then I tried shoving at it with all my might. I got another horrendous sound of complaining rust and metal, but it refused to open. I let the doorway back down and drew a deep breath. This would have to be my last try. Even with the El, the noise I was making couldn't be ignored or missed much longer.

Once more I waited for the noise of the El, one of the few times I wished rush hour would hurry up and arrive. The roar began and, once more, my back to the floor, I tried to stand. Every instant of running and working out got put into this push, along with my love for Scott. I heard a squeal, but kept pushing—and then a sudden snap, a clatter and the door burst upward, and my head bashed into a two-by-four on the underside of the floor.

For a second, I felt dizzy then touched the back of my head. My hand came away feeling wet. I didn't need to look to tell it was blood, nor would the creatures in the crawl space need to see it, either. Blood would make them even bolder. I scrambled around, stuck my head through the portal, got my shoulders through, and rested my elbows on either side for a second. I glanced around the room.

I no longer had to wonder abut what happened to Brad Stawalski. His pale and inert body lay a foot away from my left elbow. I crushed the thought out of my head of what this meant about the possibility of finding Scott alive, but tried to take reassurance that I was on the right track and this building was where Scott would be found.

I was in a laundry room with a washer and dryer that couldn't have been used since the end of the first Mayor Daley's administration. A bare bulb above a warped and peeling door emitted a feeble light. After a moment of listening, I hoisted myself up and replaced the square of floor. Once on my feet, I listened intently again. Nothing. The room required only a cursory examination. It was about ten feet square, with bare shelves on the walls. My clothes were a filth-encrusted mess. Brushing them off was useless: my hands were just as slime covered, and there wasn't time.

An oak door was the only exit besides that which I'd entered. I didn't want to think of returning to my verminous friends.

I tried the door. In the first thing that had gone right since the last Ice Age, the knob turned. I flicked down the light switch next to the door, but nothing happened. The power must be controlled from someplace else. I pulled out my hankie and used it to cover my fingers as I unscrewed the bulb.

I edged the door open, listening for any possible sound from it, or of human habitation from the other side. The wood of the door was an inch thick. I extended more care than an archaeologist entering an ancient tomb for the first time. I pulled it open far enough so that a crack gave me the beginnings of a view of the room on the other side. No humans presented themselves to my immediate range of vision.

A humming roar suddenly built to a din that awakened echoes of Vietnam in my mind. A helicopter was landing nearby. The roar turned into the whomping sound of the propeller of a helicopter winding down.

I edged the door farther open. I looked into a room with a rusting refrigerator and a sink dangling from one pipe jutting from the wall. No tables or chairs, and no doors on gaping and empty cabinets. This house must be unoccupied: that and the noise of the El must have covered the sound of my entry.

Through a window, the gray of early dawn gave me a brief look at the prospect outside. In the empty lot on the other side of the El track, I could see the rear propeller and a few inches of flying machine and the slowly rotating main propeller of the helicopter.

I opened the door an eighth of an inch at a time, listening intently and barely breathing. Nothing moved near me. Then, through the window, I saw the top halves of three men, all wearing sports jackets and grim frowns. By now I had the door open a quarter of the way. I pulled it nearly closed, but left myself a view out the window. They walked toward the left, never looking in my direction.

As soon as they were out of sight, I swung open the door and hurried to the right. Each room presented the prospect of a heavy oak door like the first one I had passed through. Each necessitated the care with which I eased through the first one. With my fear for Scott churning my nerves on fast forward, I explored the house. I don't know how I managed to keep my patience and care on slow motion. From looking out the front windows of the second room to the glow of the streetlights outside, I realized I was in the middle house. I'd either passed the entrances from below in the first house, or there weren't any.

I wondered briefly when the help that Bill Proctor said he'd send would get here. I wasn't about to wait for anyone to rescue Scott; but, at this point, a little cavalry arriving in the nick of time wouldn't have bothered me.

I explored beyond the kitchen into a dining room which led directly into what I assumed might have been a parlor or living room. I got enough light from the street lamps and near-dawn to make my way carefully, although no obstructions presented themselves in any of the rooms. Only one room had a carpet, with faded roses twirling and entwining around each other. They might have been multicolored and cheerful when the carpet was first installed, but now their tired petals and worn briars barely showed through the years of gray dust, dirt, and neglect.

I crept across each floor keeping close to the walls, hoping to eliminate any squeaks and groans in the floorboards. The homes connected at the back along what might have been a servants' entrance or corridor. I inched through this and began my exploration of the third house.

Suddenly I heard an agonized yowl. Its pure sound of animal pain and fear could not disguise that it was Scott. He was nearby and alive. This last thought kept me from racing headlong to a rescue. I wanted us to get away, not simply for me to join him in being tortured and killed.

The bellow ended in a gurgle and then a whisper of "Please stop."

The scream had been horrific, but his desperate plea, spoken in a cracked whisper, drove my fury to an icy calm waiting to explode with volcanic anger. I knew immediately that whoever wreaked this agony would pay.

I arrived at a set of parlor doors that opened to each side, rather than in or out. The house was old, and the floors had begun to sag toward the middle, preventing these doors from closing perfectly. I put my eye to the opening.

I brought my hand to my mouth. No scream could express my horror and fear. Five feet of floor separated the room I was in from the one across the hall. The doors of that room were flung wide open. Scott sat in a chair with one wrist handcuffed to a rung behind his back. His face was a bloody pulp. His sweatshirt hung in tatters down his chest. The left sleeve of Scott's sweatshirt had been ripped up. The arm with tattered cloth remnants scattered around it lay on a small table, palm down. I watched as one of the men took hold of Scott's hand and turned it over. From elbow to wrist I saw the results of cigarette burns. I smelled burnt flesh. Blood trickled down the back of his blond hair, turning it a crimson orange. Rope was looped around his chest and stomach. I could see welts on his wrists where the flesh had been bruised as he'd tried to struggle.

I saw only three guys. One turned Scott's hand over. The foot of another had a gun barrel resting on it. A third stood against the far wall smoking a cigarette and looking bored. I didn't know how many might be out of my line of sight.

The one smoking the cigarette said, "You should let me use the cattle prod on his nuts. I bet he'd jump. I like to watch them jump."

A voice—not from the two guys I could see—said, "I still think we should cut his dick off and stuff it in his mouth. I've always wanted to be the one to do that."

"Maybe later," said the one who turned Scott's hand over. He took a puff from a cigarette he'd been holding in his other hand. He blew a smoke ring toward the ceiling. Without asking questions or demanding answers, he casually placed the lit tip close to Scott's arm. The torturer examined the underside with care and precision. He seemed to be searching for a good spot to inflict the next jolt of pain.

He drew in his breath slightly, grunted, sighed, and brought the lit tip to the inside of Scott's elbow. He paused an inch above the surface. He said, as if he were having a conversation with Scott, "You see, the trick is to do it long enough to inflict the most pain, but not so long that the cigarette goes out."

He jammed the cigarette into Scott. Every muscle in my lover's body tried to pull away from the pain. A scream that could have reached the Loop rent the air.

For the next several minutes, I don't remember a conscious thought. No she-bear enraged by an attack on her cubs could have been more dangerous or deadly than I in those next few instants. I suppose it was surprise more than anything else that gave me what little advantage I had.

Probably I should have planned a diversion with more subtlety.

I took each of the doors I was behind and threw them open. Before they had a chance to look in my direction, I was in the room, with my hand on the barrel of the gun I'd seen, wrenching the weapon out of the startled creep's hand, and toppling him over backward on his chair.

The one who'd been torturing Scott reached for a long-barreled gun. Before it even swung in my direction, I put a bullet between his eyes. I didn't have time to enjoy the satisfaction of watching him collapse because the guy with the cigarette aimed his gun at me.

I leaped sideways, rammed into the table, and shoved it into his midsection. He doubled over silently. I reached across the table, grabbed his shirtfront, and bashed his head on the table. Unconscious, he slumped to the floor. The third guy jumped toward a couple of guns sitting on a table near the front window.

"Don't move!" I bellowed. He whirled to face me with an awful grin and the maw of a gigantic weapon turned in my direction. I swung to the floor, rolled, and began firing.

Somewhere in there, I realized someone was screaming and shouting furious imprecations. It dawned on me that I was the one. I fired wildly at the gunman at the front. I couldn't see where I hit him, but he collapsed to the ground, moaning.

I heard pounding footsteps coming from deeper in the house. I snatched another gun from the front table, and with one in each hand, marched to the sliding doors. I stood at the entry and poured a rain of fire from both of the guns toward the door at the far end of the room. After the booming echoes faded, I listened. No footsteps sounded, but I could hear a distant babble of confusion. I caught only snatches of "Get back! What the hell's going on! I think I'm hit!"

One gun clicked empty. I tossed it away and picked the third gun up from the table I rushed to Scott.

He was unconscious. I didn't waste time trying to rouse him. I made sure he was breathing, then untied the ropes holding him. I had no idea where the keys to the handcuffs were. I smashed the rung of the chair with the bottom of my shoe. Scott began to slump to the floor.

I held him in my arms and tried to get him up. I still hadn't heard any sounds approaching, but I knew the killers could be back anytime.

I didn't want to try the hall and the door. I didn't want to take a step closer to our pursuers. Even with two guns, I knew their firepower could easily outgun mine, and that very soon. An assault on the room had to be coming in seconds.

I carried, pulled, dragged Scott to the picture window. The drop outside was about five feet. We'd have to do it.

I began to hear sounds approaching. I looked down at the creep lying near the window. I could see his shallow breathing. His gun was near my left foot. I eased Scott out of my arms, bent down, and picked up the gun by my foot. I held two guns awkwardly in my left hand as I aimed the one in my right toward the doorway, emptied it in their direction, and tossed it away. I kept one gun in my right hand and the other in my belt.

Then I turned and shot out the glass in the window. I didn't have time for finesse. I propped Scott on the edge of the windowsill, dangling his feet in front of him. I tried to lower him, but I had no time to be careful. He slipped and tumbled to the ground. When I was halfway through the window, I looked back to see the head of a figure appear around the door. I fired a round and scrambled out the window. I just missed landing on Scott.

Not a car crept by on the deserted street. I didn't want to be exposed on the pavement for even a few seconds. I didn't know when enemies might rush out of the buildings. My truck was on the far side of the three houses. The stairs to the elevated station loomed a short half-block to my left. The only protection on the way was the pilings of the El, but I'd have to risk it. Staying here was pointless.

I picked Scott up in a fireman's carry and hefted him to my shoulder. I kept my gun arm as free as possible.

He was heavy, and I staggered under his weight. The years of forcing myself to work out when I'd rather have taken another helping of chocolate paid off now. We worked out at least three nights a week during the off season, and I continue the regimen while Scott plays in the summer. If I wasn't in good shape, this would have been hopeless. Still, if help didn't come soon, we'd never make it.

I heard guns firing behind me. I risked a glance back. No one followed, but it sounded like a firefight going on inside the houses.

I made it to the bottom of the steps to the El without being fired upon. It was still too early for rush-hour crowds to stream to work. I didn't dare rest.

Halfway up to the El platform, a train roared into the station. I surged upward and stumbled. I'd never make it before the train left. No one exited. The train started quickly, built speed, and left in a wild rush. When the noise stopped, I heard gunfire close by and the pings of shells hitting the metal of the stairs. I fired several rounds back and then forged ahead, hoping the cover of the metal pilings would be enough protection. Their battle or confusion was over, and they were after us. At least on the platform, I'd have the upper ground to withstand a siege and maybe find a way to escape. Puffing up the stairs with Scott was tough, but I had enough of a lead. I thought I'd make it before they caught up. I certainly hoped so.

I heard the helicopter start up. At the top of the stairs, the ticket taker took one look at my gun and backed away from the glass opening.

"Call the police!" I shouted.

He shook his head, held his hands up, and shooed them at me in a go-away motion. I heard the clatter of footsteps on the stairs behind me. I propped Scott against a billboard advertising condoms. He still hadn't regained consciousness.

I hid behind a metal pillar at the top of the stairs. I watched three of them creeping forward. I let them get halfway there before I took careful aim and fired three rounds. They darted backward. I could no longer afford to waste ammunition. I heard no police sirens.

I didn't bother to stare to see whether I'd hit any of them. I heard the sound of a train. I scrambled to Scott, got his left arm around my shoulder, and put my right around his waist. I pulled and dragged him the few feet to the edge of the platform.

Moments later, the two-car train pulled in. I yanked us into the second car. As the doors closed, I looked back to see two guys with guns drawn running up the last few stairs.

The train pulled out. I eased Scott into a seat. A black woman in a bright yellow shawl and a teenager in an Oakland Raiders jacket stared at us. I stuck the gun in my belt, then sat down next to Scott.

I took out my hankie and dabbed at the places where blood still oozed from Scott's head. I kept murmuring, "Wake up, Scott. Come on, lover, please." But he didn't revive, and nothing I tried brought him around. His breathing remained ragged and uneven. I felt two inches to the right of his Adam's apple. His pulse was still strong.

The black woman stepped softly close to us. Her breasts were gigantic, and her butt completely filled the aisle. "You all right?" she whispered.

The sight of me as a mud-encrusted, blood-spattered human didn't seem to faze her.

"It's my lover," I said, not caring what she thought of gay people.

The woman sat on the other side of Scott. She said, "Can I help?"

I cradled Scott's head in my arms. I didn't remember when I started to cry.

She said, "It's going to be all right." She stood up, patted me on the shoulder, marched to the front of the car, and disappeared through the connecting door to the one in front. Briefly I heard the click of the tracks louder, then softer with the door closed, then again louder moments later when she returned.

She came back and sat next to me. She said, "The motorman's called the police. They'll meet you at the next station." She put her hand on my shoulder. At the moment, that human warmth from a stranger was all the world to me.

At the next stop, she helped me maneuver Scott off the train. I'd hoped to see a swarm of uniformed cops converging on the area. I didn't want to leave the protection of the moving train with no one here to meet us. What if the drug criminals decided to pursue us from station to station? It wouldn't take them that long to hop in cars and scramble after us, but I noted that the train didn't move. Perhaps the motorman was waiting, as we were, to see what the moment held.

We struggled forward a few steps toward the stairs leading down. I loosened the gun in my belt in case it was needed. Finally I saw the top of a Chicago beat cop's hat begin to emerge from the steps. I'd never been more glad to see members of the local constabulary.

Within seconds, the glow from rotating Mars lights heralded what I chose to view as the tardy-but-welcome cavalry. In minutes, an ambulance arrived and paramedics rushed up.

They worked magnificently. The woman in charge barked a steady stream of sensible commands as the three blue-clad paramedics hunted through their oversized toolbox for medicines and cures. The rapidity and precision with which they worked gave me confidence.

The woman spoke into her hand radio: "Estimated time of arrival at your location eleven minutes." She requested a number of medical items to be available when they arrived.

Getting the stretcher down the stairs was far easier than I expected. If I'd had time for any thought besides that for Scott's health, I'd have realized that working in Chicago, it would be common for them to have to bring people down flights of stairs from two- and three-story homes and apartments.

The African-American woman held my hand for a few moments as they loaded Scott's unconscious form into the ambulance. At least no one had slipped a sheet or blanket over his face. The woman patted me several times and said, "He's going to be all right, honey." And then she was gone in the gathering crowd. I was too distracted to stop her. I never got a chance to thank her.

⊾ 10 ⊿

At the ambulance doors, I said, "I'm riding with him." No one objected. The trip to the hospital was silent except for moments when we passed over a railroad crossing. Then the person riding shotgun would say, "Tracks," and the people in back would hold Scott more steadily and hang onto an IV bottle which was already dripping into his arm.

At the hospital, they made me wait in the hall. I nearly went berserk at that rule, but the hospital personnel were firm, and the police insisted I tell them what had happened. Even that wouldn't have kept me from my lover, but one of the doctors, a man in his early thirties, said to me, "We're going to do everything we can. You can't help by getting in our way. You'll be able to see him as soon as we can allow it."

I didn't ask whether Scott would be okay. I didn't want to hear an answer I couldn't live with. The doctor's voice was low and calm and soothing, and he had piercing violet eyes that met mine unflinchingly. He disappeared through the swinging doors of the emergency room.

I got a cursory check from the emergency-room personnel. They cleaned the back of my head where I banged it getting out of the crawl space. They slapped a Band-Aid on it and gave me a tetanus shot.

Cops surrounded me, and one of them began asking questions. What I'd said at the El station had been more than enough to set them in motion to the three row houses and to guarantee a cop stayed close to me throughout the proceedings. They couldn't know for certain whether I was a suspect or good guy at the moment, and I didn't care. Nothing mattered except Scott. He had to be all right. Every time the doors back to where he was swung open, I began to rise to my feet. I wanted to see the young doctor emerge.

Bolewski and Quinn showed up a half-hour later. "What the hell happened back there?" Bolewski asked.

I stood up, advanced toward him, and gave him a look which would have stopped a herd of rampaging elephants.

He took a step back.

I said, "I saved my lover. Not you two. Not any police. Not anybody. I did." Then I began to shake. Even though I'd been in the marines, it had been twenty years, and lots of memories get buried very deep. But I had nearly been killed, and several evil people were dead at my hand, and I didn't know if Scott would live.

I sat down and clutched my arms around myself to quell the shaking, but I wasn't through with my belligerence. "Anybody wants to dispute what I say, wants to tell a different side of the story, I don't care! I care about one thing: that Scott lives."

I couldn't stop shaking. My voice was rising and breaking like a puberty-stricken adolescent. I knew I was beginning to lose it.

Quinn sat next to me. "Tom," he said, "we'd like you to take everything real slow. Just talk to us about what happened. We need to move as quickly as possible to try to catch any people who may have gotten away."

"A helicopter," I said. "They used one to arrive. Must have been somebody important. I heard it starting up as I took Scott to the train."

Quinn barked several orders to a nearby uniformed cop, who flew out of the room to call the FAA to check on all helicopter reports.

"How did you find them?" Quinn asked.

"Bill Proctor and I found the list of safe houses for Frederico Torres around the world. This was the one in Chicago."

"Why didn't you bring the information to us?" Quinn asked.

"Bill Proctor was going to. He never got to you guys?"

"No," Quinn said.

"What happened to my lawyer and the Mexican authorities?"

"Whoever grabbed them was more worried about Scott. They tried to move everybody to different cars near the Cabrini Green housing project this morning. The guards your lawyer hired managed to get everyone away except Scott. They didn't give us a lot to go on. The kidnappers seemed content with having Scott and didn't pursue the rest of them. They're lucky to be alive."

Quinn asked for more details about our discovery of the materials.

I told him about the post office and the packaging of the relics. I handed him the list, which I'd used to uncover the safe house on the South Side.

Quinn held the list more carefully than a scholar holding a fragment of the Dead Sea Scrolls. Bolewski looked over his shoulder. After a few seconds' reading, Quinn whistled. "This is incredible," he said. "How did you know he would be there?"

"I didn't." I explained about the relics, the computer disks, and the materials on Mr. and Mrs. Proctor. "That stuff on the parents could be very important. When I left him, Bill was supposed to be taking all that material to the authorities. I'm worried about him."

"Why didn't you bring it to us?" Bolewski asked.

"Because I wasn't going to waste a second waiting for the cops, whether it was warrants, or due process, or assembling SWAT teams to attack. They might have used

Scott as a hostage. You people haven't been the most helpful."

A uniformed cop trundled his bulk into the room. He spoke to Quinn. "Lots of press outside. The Scott Carpenter baseball thing is on the radio. They want information."

Quinn said, "Maybe a statement later. They'll want to stampede to the crime scene when they get word of that. Gonna be a hell of a day."

The doctor came out of the emergency room. I rose to my feet. My trembling, which had eased somewhat during the questioning, returned.

"Are you Tom?" the doctor asked.

I nodded.

"He's asking for you. We usually only let family in, but he insisted."

"Is he going to be okay?"

"He should be all right," the doctor said. "We want to keep him here for observation at least overnight. Besides the obvious external injuries, he's got a concussion and may have other internal injuries. He was beat up pretty bad. You can see him now."

Quinn and Bolewski left.

The doctor led me through the emergency-room doors to where he pulled back a sliding curtain. Scott's eyes were open. The last quarter-inch of his mouth on the right—the only part not puffed and bruised—rose in a slight grin. He lifted two fingers in greeting. The doctor left.

I took his hand and with the other caressed his brow, moving his hair back.

"I don't feel good," he whispered.

"I love you," I said. "I love you more than anything in the world."

His hand gripped tighter in mine. "Am I going to be okay?"

"The doctor said yes."

"What happened?" he asked.

I told him everything that I'd done since he'd been taken, then asked, "What did they do to you?"

He breathed quietly for a minute. He had two small hoses running to his nostrils. They had him hooked up to a couple of machines. One I figured had to be heart rate and one blood pressure but I wasn't sure. A few shelves carried medical paraphernalia of use to someone, but incomprehensible to me.

"Mostly I was at that house, I think," Scott said. "My arm hurts."

I looked at the bandages where I'd seen his left arm burned deep with cigarettes.

"Do you want me to get them to give you more painkillers?" I asked.

"I want you to stay close," he said.

"Do you want anything, need anything?"

He shook his head slightly. His eyelids nodded, closed, then opened abruptly, then began to shut again. While still holding his hand, I gently caressed his arm, shoulder, forehead.

His eyes fought with his brain to drift into sleep.

"Everything's okay now," I said. "You're safe now."

He shut his eyes. I felt his body relax, and in a few minutes, the grip on my hand began to loosen. I leaned over and gently kissed his forehead.

Without opening his eyes, he murmured, "I love you."

I stayed with him for several hours. I found out later that time limits on visiting were pretty flexible. Mostly he slept. During Scott's transfer to intensive care, I had to wait in the hall, but Quinn and Bolewski were back, and they gave me answers to questions that I had. Quinn was actually pretty nice about the whole thing.

I was exhausted from lack of sleep and the physical and emotional exertion. I'd gotten several cans of orange juice from the cafeteria, and so far that had sustained me.

"What did you find on the South Side?" I asked.

"The scene was a mess," Quinn said. "The crime-lab guys have been at it for hours. We've got five dead bodies, including Frederico and his brother Pedro Torres. One of the ones you shot is dead. The other one will probably live. The helicopter never got off the ground. Three of the survivors have begun to talk."

"Who kidnapped Scott?" I asked.

"Pedro. It seems that the people chasing you got conflicting orders. Pedro's the one who wanted you alive. That's probably why the people with you when Scott was kidnapped didn't get chased. If it had been Frederico, they'd probably all be dead."

"Why torture Scott?" I asked.

"They wanted information."

"Which he couldn't possibly give them," I said.

"Glen Proctor really screwed things up," Quinn said. "He must have been awful busy in Mexico to accomplish all this in just a couple of weeks."

"I bet he'd been planning his schemes for a while," I said. "Have you found Bill?"

"Not yet."

"Do his parents know anything?" I asked.

"Neither mother nor father claims to have seen him," Quinn said.

"Liars!"

"Glen was playing a dangerous game," Quinn said. "I hope Bill's not caught up in it."

"What was the big fight about on the South Side?" I asked.

"You started that."

"I did?"

"You did. That helicopter you heard was the arrival of Frederico Torres himself. He was set to have a big meeting with his brother. Negotiations had been going on since Glen Proctor, posing as Scott Carpenter, had managed to steal the information about all the safe houses, plus other shipments, dealers, and major distributors. Pedro had

180

thought Glen was just after his brother, but it seems Glen was trying to double-cross him, too. Glen had some information on Pedro, too. Glen was trying to either double-cross both of them or extort money from both. Everybody was after Glen. Frederico just wanted him dead because he'd ruined their plans. He wanted vengeance. He knew he'd have to move his entire operation. He figured that Pedro would have the information in a short time, and probably all the international police jurisdictions. Even somebody that rich has to worry at that point. Pedro wanted Glen alive long enough to talk to him."

"So the ones after us who wanted to kill—"

"Were Frederico's men," Quinn finished for me. "They just wanted you dead."

"There were two groups of guys trying to chase us outside our place that morning," I said. "They came from different sides of the building. One crowd didn't shoot because they wanted to talk. The other wanted to kill us."

"That sounds right," Quinn said.

"So, if they were shooting, they were Frederico's guys, and if not, they were Pedro's?"

"Sort of," Quinn said. "Let me finish about the battle," Quinn said.

I was silent.

"The meeting between them was all set. Negotiations had been delicate because neither side trusted the other, but they knew they had to confront each other. When you started firing while you were rescuing Scott, the bodyguards on both sides figured that the truce was being broken. An enormous firefight broke out."

"You wouldn't believe what those houses look like," Bolewski said.

"Combat zone hardly describes it. Those guys have incredible firepower. Think of how much damage you did with the few weapons you had in that room. They let loose at each other with everything they had."

"We walked through the houses," Bolewski said. "Walls

sagged because they'd been riddled with so many bullets. Stairways collapsed from having so much lumber shot away. These guys used big guns." Bolewski seemed to relish the whole concept. "Made the St. Valentine's Day Massacre look like the peanut gallery having a spat."

Quinn said, "It wasn't pretty. Five dead, like I said. A few wounded, and the three who are talking to us. The fight was winding down when the cops started arriving. Fortunately, the first cops who showed up had the sense not to approach. They knew this wasn't some simple gang war."

"How did the police put a stop to it?" I asked.

"We didn't," Quinn said. "By the time we had the area secured, the El trains stopped, the streets blocked, and whatever else was needed, the shooting had stopped. They weren't firing at us to begin with, and what was the point? So many of them were dead, and we had half the cops in the city outside there after a while. Those left alive inside knew it was pointless to try to shoot their way out."

"Are Scott and I still going to be in danger?" I asked.

"With both Frederico and Pedro dead," Quinn said, "I doubt it."

"Frederico looked like Swiss cheese," Bolewski said. "I made sure I got up close to see him. I wanted to be able to tell my grandkids."

"There isn't much of an organization left to chase you," Quinn said. "Those three gave us all this information. All of them are going to be in jail in this country forever, and if enough time ever passes for them to be out of jail, then they'll be sent back to South America for more trials. They don't care about Scott Carpenter or Tom Mason anymore. Nobody cares anymore."

"So Frederico's guys killed Glen Proctor," I said.

"*That* none of the three knew for sure or would admit at this point," Quinn said. "Probably some of the dead guys executed him."

We'd been sitting in a small conference room with modern fixtures and comfortable chairs. I was tired from lack of sleep and spent emotions. Someone knocked on the door and a young cop stuck his head in the room. He whispered briefly to Quinn, then left.

Quinn said, "Your lawyer's here." It was nearly noon. We met Todd, who was dressed impeccably, as always. A woman named Debra McKenna was with him. We trudged to the cafeteria where I guzzled more orange juice and wolfed down an omelet. We exchanged stories about our adventures, then Todd said, "Debra is my accountant. She has found more information. She and I have been working together since I got her out of bed at five this morning." She wore a beige skirt, white blouse, and a blue blazer. Her briefcase was five inches thick and solid black. She opened it and pulled out three folders.

"I have more information on the Proctors. The government has been watching both people for some time," Debra said. "Each has been under investigation. Mr. Proctor is thought to have been bribing a slew of Mexican government employees. It is highly illegal to bribe foreign officials. It cost one company nearly ten million in fines not more than a few years ago, and they lost a great deal of their business. So that kind of evidence is going to hurt him. He'll have to go to trial, of course, and it will take years. While the fines he'll have to pay aren't as critical as they would be to ordinary mortals, the loss of business will at least cramp his style. We've also been tracking down rumors of Mrs. Proctor being involved in an illegal banking scheme that would make the BCCI mess look like the local five-and-dime. The whole labyrinthine scheme is complicated even more because both Proctors spent huge amounts of time, money, and resources obfuscating their own and each other's work."

"Mother and Father are fierce competitors," I said. "They hate each other. They are desperate to hurt one another. They'd have sold a nursing home full of grandparents to get their way. Maybe Glen was double-crossing both of them too." I explained about the information Bill Proctor had.

"The data he has could probably really hurt them," she said.

"Won't the Mexican government want to do something about the relics we found?" I asked.

"If the Proctors were involved, the Mexican government is not in the business of offending fabulously wealthy American businesspeople who might invest millions in their country. They are happy to get the relics back, fake or real. They are more happy to get the jobs. Remember, they aren't that eager to prosecute for bribing their officials. It is against American laws, and they'll be prosecuted in American courts."

"Bill Proctor said his mother and father were supposed to have had some kind of big powwow," I said. "If they're going to get together here, I'd like to get an invitation to that."

"Don't do something illegal," Todd warned.

I told him I wouldn't.

Debra and Todd left.

I asked the cops, "If Glen was using an alias and they killed him, why did they chase us after they found the body in the penthouse?"

"We don't know if whoever got there first thought they were killing Scott Carpenter or Glen Proctor. The second group saw you run. Did they know who killed Glen? If they looked at identification and saw Glen Proctor and they were after Scott Carpenter, would that change what they did? We'll probably never be sure. A lot depends on who could recognize Proctor. We just don't know who got there first. The second group was probably Pedro's men, and they hadn't killed the dead guy, and they didn't know who you were. You didn't stay to answer questions. They may have chased you simply to talk to you, or they may have thought you had specific knowledge and they wanted to kill you. The guys who are talking are being helpful, but very careful. Their lawyers are with them, so it's a very touchy situation."

"Who came and got the body, and why?" I asked. "And if it wasn't the killers, how did whoever came know it was there?"

Even with these unanswered questions, none of the official folks wanted to pursue Glen's death. They had buckets full of suspects on the South Side, all dead. Without a body, there wasn't a lot to work with. Besides, they had a perfect explanation with the biggest drug kingpins on two continents dead in the city morgue. "The Proctor murder was a case of mistaken identity," Bolewski said. "Be glad it wasn't you, and forget it."

The cops left.

I visited with Scott. He was awake, and I gave him all the news. But he was tired and I was exhausted. After a while, he pressed the button on the side of the bed to lower it. When it reached a comfortable spot he took his finger off the control, leaned back, and shut his eyes.

I thought I'd sit in the chair for a while before going home. After a few minutes, I'd begun to nod off when a nurse came in. She had a puzzled expression on her face.

"This just came for Scott Carpenter or Tom Mason," she said. She looked at Scott. "I know who he is, but who's Mason?"

"I am," I said.

She gave me the envelope.

"Where'd this come from?" I asked.

"One of those messenger services," she said. She left.

Inside the envelope was a message from Bill Proctor. It didn't say where he was, but it did say that he had a meeting with his parents at the North Shore mansion late this afternoon. He asked me to be there. I realized he couldn't have called. Because of the multitude of media, we'd had the phone turned off in Scott's room.

The cops had brought my pickup truck to the hospital.

I stopped in the cafeteria and drank three more cans of orange juice, which revived me enough for the moment.

Lake Shore Drive, Sheridan Road, all the wealth of the north suburbs were a blur as I sped to the Proctors'. It was late afternoon, and the rush-hour traffic was heavy.

When I got there, I wasn't about to knock and ask permission to enter. I drove to a hundred feet from the front entrance. I set the truck in gear and jumped out. I then climbed the wall, jumped down to the other side, and strolled to the front door. I figured they had some kind of surveillance on the grounds, but I hoped the diversion of the truck smashing into the gate and my determination would get me through.

Actually, I got as far as the liveried servant and the front door before several armed security guards in green army fatigues showed up. I grabbed James, the butler, and used him as a buffer for the few seconds it took to get inside.

"Where are they?" I said.

"I'm sure I don't know what you mean," he said.

Not bad for a guy with an arm around his windpipe. I flung him outside and slammed the door, then raced to the grand staircase.

I took the stairs three at a time. They'd have to figure out where I'd gone. This seemed my quickest way out of anybody's line of sight. Seconds after I reached the top, I heard wild scrambling and feet pounding behind me on the marble floor, then the softer thud of boots thumping on the carpet up the stairs after me.

For a few seconds, I felt as if I was in one of those Marx Brothers comedies, or maybe the Three Stooges, with doors opening and slamming shut and characters rushing in and out.

I managed to get back to the first floor to a room that opened onto a patio outside some French windows before a machine-gun-toting kid, maybe all of eighteen, met me coming in a door I was going out. He leveled the trembling gun in my direction.

A door opened behind me.

"What is this?" Jason Proctor's voice said.

I swiveled my head around, and the kid poked the muzzle of his gun into my chest. I stepped back.

Mr. Proctor approached.

"We're going to talk," I said.

He glared at me.

"Get rid of him," Proctor said. "If you have to, shoot him."

"Is that how Glen died?" I asked. "You just gave an order, and the boys took care of it for you?"

He walked up to me swiftly and slapped me hard.

"Not happy about the truth?"

I caught his hand the next time he raised it, but my soldier buddy whapped me on the side of the head with his gun.

I barely felt it. The adrenaline poured through my body.

Mrs. Proctor walked into my field of vision from the back of the room.

"Jason!" Her voice was sharp.

The three of us looked at her as she marched across the room.

"We'll discuss this like civilized people!"

By this point, a large contingent of servants and guards had arrived.

"Go!" Mrs. Proctor commanded. One word, and they went. "Bill is in the library," she said. She led us to a room with floor-to-ceiling bookcases lined with books that all had golden spines and embossed lettering.

Three groups of black leather chairs sat from the front of the room to the back: one at the door, one in the middle, and one at the far end. In one of the black leather chairs in the middle of the room, Bill Proctor sat. He wore a white fisherman's sweater, dark blue jeans and white socks and gym shoes. He barely looked at me. Mrs. Proctor wore a beige wool pant suit. Mr. Proctor was in a blue blazer, white shirt, duck trousers, and penny loafers.

Mrs. Proctor pointed at me. "Why is this person here?"

"Because he was honest with me. Because I trust him. Because I want him here," Bill said. He glared at his mother.

With practiced grace, she shrugged off his tone and aggressiveness and indicated seats. I took the chair across from Bill, and Mr. Proctor sat to my right. Mrs. Proctor told her husband she didn't want a chair.

She stood in the center of the Oriental carpet that nearly touched the bookcases around the edges.

"Where have you been?" I asked Bill.

He picked up a briefcase from next to his chair. He clicked the locks open and spilled the contents onto the rug.

"What's the meaning of this?" Mr. Proctor asked.

"Oh, bluster out your ass, Jason!" Mrs. Proctor said.

"Where's Glen's body?" Bill asked.

"How dare you?" Jason asked.

"How dare I, Dad? I'll tell you how. I've been using the past twelve hours to have all the materials on the disks transcribed and analyzed. It cost me a small fortune, but I learned how to spend from both of you. Besides being a record of all that Glen had been up to, it was a record of what you and your companies have been doing."

Bill was breathing heavily and his fists clenched and unclenched.

"Now son," Mr. Proctor started.

"I'm going to do all the talking," Bill said.

"Shut up and let him," Mrs. Proctor said.

"You keep silent, too, Mom!" Bill said.

Mouth agape, she plopped abruptly into a chair.

Bill picked up a sheaf of papers from the floor. "Glen explained everything in code on paper or on the computer disks. First the necklaces. That was a lark he got into just two weeks ago. He's worked with the drug people for a while, but he just got the information on them about two months ago, the final details a few days before he was killed. The relic stealing was a fluke. Brad Stawalski got some hot stuff he couldn't get rid of. He knew Glen had connections. Brad didn't tell the truth. Neither of you thought Glen could ever make plans and carry them out, but he did. I know that a lot of what he did was to con people. He took precautions when dealing with the drug people, like using a fake name." Bill tossed the papers he'd been holding in a heap on the floor. He wiped his hands across his face.

Both of his parents started to speak.

"Be silent!" he shouted at them. "Just for once in your lives, shut the fuck up!" The fury and anger in his tone and the glare of his eyes pierced through their consciousness and held them dumb.

"The rest of the information on the disks was about you two. Glen wasn't just trying to get dirt on you guys. He actually seemed to be trying to be part of both companies. He desperately wanted you to respect him. Even more, Glen the joker, the wild one, always desperately wanted the two of you to get along. We used to talk about it. He wanted no more fights. All that acting out he did as a kid was a way to try and get your attention off each other and onto himself. Glen hadn't changed much."

"I knew he wouldn't do anything illegal against us," Mrs. Proctor managed to get in.

"He was getting dirt, and it was illegal," Bill said. "He was in Mexico bribing people to screw Dad out of projects you, Mom, had bribed people to sabotage. These people picked up triple bribes. They must have thought they'd latched onto the lost treasure of El Dorado. And, speaking of bribes, he got some great information out of your banking people, Mom." Bill barked a one-note harsh laugh that jarred all of my teacher instincts. He continued, "And Glen was using money from both of your companies to bribe everybody. Maybe he thought it would be something of a lark to screw up both of your companies. You know how wild and crazy he was. Who knows what he may have actually been planning?"

Bill shut his eyes and leaned back in the chair.

Both parents spoke at once. Bill let it go on for several minutes as each parent got louder and louder. Suddenly he opened his eyes and leaned forward. As his parents each drew a breath, he said, "Shut up." Speaking the words softly, as he did, had an enormous impact.

We sat in silence. The grandfather clock near the door chimed seven o'clock. I wanted to go home and sleep for days.

Bill said to me, "What did the police find out? I heard snatches of news about what happened on the South Side."

I told him what happened. "What the cops don't know— and once again are ignoring—is who killed Glen. I know the relic people never got close enough to kill anybody. The necklace people got what they wanted. That leaves the drug people and you three. There were two sides in the drug war: pro- and anti-Frederico." I explained what the cops had pieced together.

I finished, "My guess is by the time either one of them got to the penthouse, Glen was already dead. I tend to think it was Pedro who got there and who chased us first because they didn't fire at us as quickly. The cops just think it's settled because they've got all these dead drug dealers, but I think it went beyond that. I think both gangs attacked us the next morning. They may have begun to think things were truly strange when they were chasing another guy who looked like Glen. Maybe he thought Glen had told us something. Maybe he thought Scott was Glen; or, as turned out to be true, they thought he sent us something. All that means is that some of the drug people didn't know or weren't satisfied with one death. Maybe Frederico wanted to eliminate anybody connected with Glen. Remember that fanatics killed the guy who translated Salman

Rushdie's work into Japanese. Just because he translated it. If Frederico was mad, who knows? But I don't think the drug people got to Glen. I think somebody else got there first." I glared at the assembled Proctors. "The question is: which one of you knew Glen was in town? He didn't make any calls while we were around. Which one of you did he call? What did he say? He was probably blackmailing both of you. Who was he going to take a bite out of first and most? Who had the most to lose? Who would order the murder of his or her own child?"

Jason Proctor stood up and took a step toward me.

I rose, as did Bill. The son forestalled his father's progress.

"You killed him!" Bill said. "Your rivalry killed him. Somehow I knew it would come to this."

"How dare you accuse your mother and me of having anything to do with your brother's death? Certainly we have been tough when it comes to business. You either get tough or lose, but we'd never try and hurt our own son. If what you say about what he found out is true, then we will have to take action immediately to minimize our loses. There was no blackmail."

"That rivalry gave you a fabulous home," Mrs. Proctor said. "And a life with chances and privileges that few people ever have. You must turn over to us all the information you have immediately."

Bill paced the floor between the chairs. "You two are the most disgusting people on the face of the planet! This family is so screwed up. Your son is dead, and all you can think of is saving your ass or defending the rivalry between the two of you. All either Glen or I wanted was your love."

They stared at him silently, as if the words had been spoken before and they were used to them, or there was truth in them and it held them dumb, or that no matter how much hurt was in them nothing could touch them, because they were rich and different.

Bill resumed, "People come to this house with ghastly news, and I'm not told. Why is that, Father? You had something to hide from the beginning. I called you, Mother, and you said you knew nothing. Either one of you had the power and strength to get a body moved and hide it. Which one of you killed my brother?"

"No one killed him," Jason Proctor said.

"Then how did he get dead?" Bill asked.

The two parents gazed at each other. Mrs. Proctor's eyes became moist. "It was a horrible accident," she said.

"Orders were given in Mexico to find Glen," Mr. Proctor said. "Our people kept running across the name 'Scott Carpenter' as someone nosing into our affairs. We never dreamed Glen was using that name. Both of our people had orders to stop Scott Carpenter at all costs and to bring Glen home. We sent private guards from here to help out."

"Not all of them knew Glen by sight." Mrs. Proctor spoke slowly.

"Our guards here do, of course," Jason said. "But the Mexican people didn't. They followed who they thought was Scott Carpenter to his place in Chicago. They were half a day behind him. The people we sent to help search were also close behind, but Glen was good at wriggling out of tight spots. He called both of us to announce he wanted to meet with us at that penthouse."

Mrs. Proctor said, "He didn't want to meet here, or at any of the offices. He wanted us alone on neutral ground. He told us he had succeeded and that we would be proud of him for the first time."

"It took over an hour to drive down from here. By then he was dead. Mason and Carpenter had been chased off. We found the body. At first we thought the drug people had got him. We had no idea who'd done it, but we didn't want a scandal. We organized the cleaning and removal. We set up internal investigations of all our security personnel. I allowed Mason and Carpenter into the house the next day to see whether they knew anything substantial."

Mrs. Proctor said, "We've barely slept. We sent our people everywhere south of the border to track information on the drug lords because we thought they'd killed him. We got nowhere. Finally we received information from our operatives that they'd killed Scott Carpenter. We knew then that a horrible mistake had been made."

"When did you find this out?" I asked.

"We've gotten bits of information all weekend. The people chasing Glen from Mexico reported to their superiors there."

"You knew Monday when we talked to you," I said to Mrs. Proctor.

"I don't answer to you," she said.

"You ordered them to kill Scott Carpenter?" I asked.

"Accidents happen," Mrs. Proctor said.

"You see," Jason Proctor said, "it was all an accident. It was nobody's fault."

Bill Proctor's laugh was long and unhealthy. The kind of laugh that you rushed to the phone to call in a team of therapists when you heard it.

"An accident!" he roared. He pointed his right index finger at his parents, accusing, fixing them in place. "Nobody's fault!" The laughter pealed again.

Mrs. Proctor stood up and reached a hand toward her son. "Bill," she said.

But he laughed again. He stooped to his briefcase, flicked it open, and came up with an enormous gun. The hole in Mr. Proctor's chest was geysering before I could leap to my feet. Mrs. Proctor's scream was cut short by a bullet in her throat. I was halfway to Bill when he raised the gun to his temple, shut his eyes, and pulled the trigger.

I heard pounding feet, so I knew I didn't have to shout for help. I knelt next to each in turn, starting with Bill. The blood was awful. My feelings of pity and terror kept me numb. I thought it might be possible to save Mrs. Proctor. Mister and Bill were beyond any help.

She died on the operating table two hours later.

I don't remember much about the interrogation by the police. I do know that Todd, my lawyer, showed up. He got me out of there in a reasonable amount of time. I know I called Scott that night before I went to sleep and told him everything. I also called school and explained what had happened and told them I wouldn't be in the next day, either. The principal was very understanding. I slept for eighteen hours.

A month later, we sat in the breakfast nook of the penthouse. Scott's wounds had healed, although he'd have permanent scars on his left arm. We were almost back to our normal level of workouts as Scott's body got back into shape. Spread out over the butcher-block tabletop were the plans for my new house in the suburbs, which would be built on what I would be able to afford from my salary.

"I like this," he said.

These were the final drawings of the plans. Building would begin in a few weeks.

"It's beautiful," I said. "It'll be like we always had it. A place to stay in the city and a place out near where I work." Scott grabbed my hand and pulled me over to him. I stretched over the top of the table so our lips met.